The Wreck

KYLE KEITH

"It's a long, arduous road he's starting to travel, but it may be that at the end of it he'll find what's he's seeking." – W. Somerset Maugham

I

Kane sat in the pale tan sand, his arms wrapped around his knees in the shade of the tree line, deep in thought. He gazed over the soft blues and greens of the ocean as the waves rolled gently into shore. The day was blissful in its calm and was now nearly over.

As he stared, Kane pondered how the choices one made in life could so directly impact their future. He considered more than just the obvious points, too. Of course, if you choose to be a sailor and one day find yourself on a ship at sea, it should not come as much of a surprise. No, he meant the little choices, the everyday decisions we take no notice of which shape who we become as people. They work as miniscule points of an immense, invisible mathematic equation that continues unending until ultimately, we end. An endless series of happenings and experiences, like dominoes toppling in perfect sequence over a line that stretches over the horizon.

Kane glanced over at the lanky, figure lying in the fetal position beside him. His name was Bell, his surname anyway, and he lay with his back to the immense jungle behind them. The wilderness seemed, from where they sat, a lush, diverse drapery of branches, leaves, and vines whose purpose appeared to be to conceal whatever might lie only mere feet from their position. In his mind's eye Kane often envisioned a large and terrible creature stalking them just out of eyeshot, and thought of how *close* that distance could indeed be.

Kane could not see the young man's youthful face, burnt nose, or his lively green eyes, though today they were anything if lively, as his long, matted, oak-brown hair covered the sharp jawline of his face in his misery. The man had the sort of hair that demanded confining in a ponytail, but he had clearly given up the social norm to bother. In fact, he had given up many social norms, even sitting up.

Kane looked back over the water. The light in the sky was now beginning to dim as the sun set far to the west behind them, somewhere beyond the wilderness. What kinds of everyday, little decisions had led him to *this* godforsaken place? He admitted he knew the recent ones. Sure he did. Those became clear enough these last few days. But what about before that? Was it the situations he had experienced, his own personal poor choices, or a patchwork of both that led him here? Before he could follow this train of thought any further, however, Bell rolled over with a groan and interrupted him.

"We're going to die, aren't we?" Bell asked in quiet defeat, almost speaking more to himself than to Kane. He stared out at the subdued dusting of colors left in the sky, looking without seeing. "That's what you're thinking there, so silent, isn't it? We're going to die here on this cursed, awful beach."

Kane sat stunned a moment, ripped out of the depths and wanderings of his mind to meet the young man's overwhelmed face. In an instant he felt infuriation course through his veins at the wretchedness of the man's look, and Kane's face lit up angry under the oranges and reds of the sunset.

"Don't be pathetic," he snapped. "And grow the hell up! Where's that attitude going to get us? We're not going to die. Not here, not today anyhow." Kane muttered the last words.

Bell was taken aback at Kane's wrath, and a gleam of coherence shone over his face from his moment of weakness.

"I'm sorry, I'm sorry. You're right. We're going to do our best. I just hate it when the night comes is all… It's the night I can't stand." His thin, patchy beard and sand-speckled hair sat in sad clumps across his face, with only the red of his nose glowing through.

Kane's anger subsided at this sad sight, and was replaced instead with pity. The night bothered him, too. It was eerie when the ability to see went away. His ears picked up all sorts of noises and his imagination ran with each individual sound. Whether the things he thought he heard were real or not, his mind would weave a fabric of possibilities of each sound's creator, racing and swirling with theories. This vicious cycle would continue until, unable to worry any longer, he would finally collapse into sleep. It was at night, Kane thought, when you were truly alone. When the reality of the situation, of *all* the situations you were confronted with, really sunk in.

"I know, I know. I hate it too," he said gruffly. He could see Bell look over at him in the dying light.

"Do you still think someone will come?" Bell asked, as the red in the sky lifted, and was overcome by faded pastels of blue and purple. The dark waves broke smoothly against the sand as the men sat, their sorry ragged clothes and unkempt selves becoming less and less visible.

It was a good question. That was the plan these past few days. They had constructed a thatched roof of dried palm leaves, which they tied to low branches as a form of shelter. During the day, they foraged the surrounding wilds for fruit with the hope someone would come. The more time went on, however, the more the unwanted idea that no one would appear seemed to bury itself relentlessly into Kane's mind, like a termite chewing its way into his head. They should have been here by now, and much as he had hoped every day that a ship would appear on the horizon, it never did. Nothing did.

"I don't know," Kane answered, scratching the beard on his chin. "Perhaps we should begin to move tomorrow. It's been days and no one has come. Help could be right over there, for all we know." He pointed in the dark to the far jutting point in the coastline to their left. Bell looked in the direction Kane pointed, as if the silhouette of a ship would reveal itself at any moment.

"But, if we left, where would we head? Which direction? We don't even know where we are and we could be heading in the opposite direction from help. I don't... I think we should stay put. We could leave and be deep in some jungle somewhere when help finally comes and we would miss it. We already have this shelter, too, and food enough for a couple more days."

"Aye... I know, I know. I know we have the shelter and the food and everything, but they should be here! And where are they? I don't know. I don't know what to do, and we could go in circles all night trying to decide."

"But, then if we stay," Bell wondered aloud, running his fingers through his hair, "we might have savages or Spaniards find us and do god only knows what to us. But if we leave, we might run into them that way, too…"

"Circles, Bell. I said we would only run in circles on this subject. Look, there's no point in worrying ourselves tonight. Tomorrow morning we'll make a plan, but tonight let's just sleep."

"But, do you know–" Bell began but Kane pounced on his words.

"I don't know, Bell, I just don't know! It's too late and I can't think clearly. Not tonight. Tomorrow we'll decide and that will be that," Kane resolved with a force in his voice, and hoped the man would let the conversation die for the night. He saw Bell turn towards him, ready to say something, but the words thankfully lodged in the man's throat and he remained silent.

The light steadily waned, and just a shaving of light and color lay resting on the horizon while the surroundings on the beach became nearly black. The moon rose over the sea, exactly where the sun had that morning, pale yellow against the deep hues of the sky. Kane slapped his knee as he felt an insect bite him. Behind them, the jungle came alive as night arose, when the birds of the day conceded their domineering sounds to the frogs and insects of the night. The volume of the jungle increased with the dying light, every minute louder than that before it. The loud choir of insects played their array of peculiar, alien sounds, and the frogs accompanied with an uneasy assortment of multi-pitched croaks. At its base, the insect song of the jungle was a droning hum, stacked with infinite layers of notes – loud buzzes, rattles, hisses and other sounds so foreign and strange Kane could not guess its maker. Geckos crawled under the roof of their shelter to exclaim a loud series of chirps before scuttling silently away to continue their hunt. A band of monkeys in the nearby hills let loose deep, guttural howls, which seemed could only have come from the lungs of unearthly demons. Others soon answered them, further in the darkness of the jungle, with howls just as terrible.

Bell was now just a silhouette, as the eyes fought to adjust to the night.

"Goodnight," he murmured.

"G'night," Kane replied, as he heard Bell shuffle to try and make himself comfortable on the dried palm leaves that made up the floor of their simple hut.

As much as Kane had hoped to leave the troubles

of the day till morning, his mind had other plans. The options they faced raged round his head like a hurricane. Should they stay, and risk not leaving, or leave, and risk having not stayed? What if the Spaniards or the savages or god knows who found them? What would they do? What *could* they do? How long could they survive? What if they ran out of food and drinkable water?

Kane began to listen closer to the noises around them, especially when a new one entered the routine, making his ears perk and his attention taut. What if a snake came in the night? Or a poisonous spider? Or a blood-thirsty jungle cat? With each thought the sounds became sharpened in his ears as they worked to distinguish each one of the seemingly hundreds.

Kane lay in the blackness of the night and listened and worried, and worried and listened, until finally he began to tire to the point of slipping off to sleep. Just before he did, however, he let his worries fall and began to simplify the otherwise impossible thoughts and dilemmas of the day. Like mud settling in a lake after a storm, his mind held one last conviction – no one was coming for them. No one.

Only then was Kane pulled away, like water in a current, off into sleep. Yet, as always those nights, it was an uneasy sleep. There it was, the smoke and the acrid smell of gunpowder hanging heavy as it enveloped him in billowing clouds. His heart began beating wildly and he was back again, hearing the cracking of pistols and rifles overhead, and the roaring of men clambering aboard the ship. Somewhere, near but out of sight, a woman's chilling scream filled the air.

II

Kane awoke the following morning and scoured the sand and dirt that speckled his hair and stuck, as if glued, to his face, arms and legs. He scratched furiously at the bites the insects had left on him throughout the night, crawled out of the woven-leaf shelter and stepped out onto the beach. Though he had fallen asleep on the leaf-strewn floor, he often tossed up that floor in his sleep to awake on the dirt and sand their hut stood on.

Kane checked his right arm as he did every morning, assessing his deep gash and the scrapes he had received nearly a week before in the ocean. The cut was no longer the bloody wound it had been, but instead had a mottled, stretched appearance, with black, dried blood at its center. The injuries were healing well, yet still he worried unendingly of infection. Were infection to strike his arm out here, in this wilderness… He didn't want to think about that.

His surroundings looked as they had every morning since his arrival – calm, tranquil, even meditative, as the gentle waves came in and out in a soft rhythm. So very unlike that fateful night. A light scent of salt from the sea hung in the gentle humidity of the morning air. Spindly little crabs skittered across the beach as the water receded from its nightly position, working tirelessly, crumble of sand at a time, to burrow into their new homes. Shame they were too small to eat, thought Kane, or he and Bell might never go hungry.

Much as Kane fretted throughout the day, the morning had a kind of magic to it that made him temporarily forget his troubles. The sun rose lazily over the sea, casting a light on the trees and greenery from such a low angle that, momentarily, all was aglow. Night had relinquished its kingdom to day, and the chorus of insects and frogs gave way to the sundry pitches and tunes of the many tropical birds. Some rattled the wilderness with their obnoxious cries, while others sang the loveliest of songs, untouched in their beauty by the greatest of human voices.

Kane stared down at the young man as he slept like the dead with his face down in the earth, much to Bell's great displeasure every time he awoke. Kane slumped and slid back against the trunk of a tree on the edge of the shoreline.

God, he thought, did the man have fears. Crushing fears that seemed to keep him here, frozen. How would Bell take it when he told him he had made up his mind to leave? The idea of staying frightened Bell as well, Kane knew, but it was a fear the man understood. Leaving would be going into the unknown, a notion that gripped Bell so strongly with terror that most times when Kane mentioned it, he was hardly able to speak. It was far more than just whether to leave or to stay that daunted Bell. Last night the man had been quiet, but on previous ones Kane had woken many times to Bell asking what a particular sound could be. Or, during the day when they foraged for food, Bell would panic and begin talking of starvation, disease, or whatever dreadful thought the cluster of distress that was his mind put forward first.

Maybe having Bell along was more trouble than it was worth, Kane considered. Meeting him seemed like a blessing at first. He had been alone after the wreck, and the trials of the day were far more difficult to face that way. In fact, when he had made his way to this beach only days ago and found Bell sitting exactly here, he was so filled with joy he could have cried. He had felt so assured then that together they would be stronger and conquer any obstacles they encountered.

Now, however, the man seemed to exist purely to pass these fears of his on to Kane. Kane understood the man's fears, of course. They existed each and every one of them deep down inside of him, too. The man was also still in many ways a youth, he knew, as he was no different at that age himself.

Bell suddenly rustled. Hacking, he sat up and scrubbed his face with his hands, spitting to get the dirt and sand out of his mouth.

"This again! Every morning! I *hate* this place," Bell spat, his face perfectly sour in the morning light.

Though on any other morning Kane would have laughed at the sight, on this particular one he found himself too invested on persuading Bell to leave their beach behind. Mocking the man would be no support. Of course, I leave regardless, Kane thought. He did not need Bell, he knew. In fact, with his moods the man may even hinder him. Yet still there was a part of him, irrespective of Bell's shortcomings, that knew he would be more comfortable should Bell join him. It was because of this that he decided to attempt to raise the man's spirits.

"Oh, come now, it's a beautiful morning, the Spaniards have not blasted us to hell, and the savages have left the hair on our heads where it belongs," Kane said smiling. Bell nodded, rubbing the sleep from his eyes.

"Then God is watching over us, even in this place," he said. This was another thing that Kane typically would have rebuked, but again he let even this go. Bell then gave him a sideways look. "Do the savages take scalps here? Like they do in America?" Kane shrugged at this.

"I have no idea what they do here. Nor how many the Spaniards even left alive since the bastards got here." Upon thinking on the subject a little more, Kane mused, "who knows, maybe they take hands here instead?"

Bell turned a shade paler and wrapped his arms around himself. Idiot, Kane thought, always rambling like an idiot and now the man is even more afraid.

"Doesn't matter," Kane waived his hand in dismissal. "That's not what's important. What *is* important is that today we leave this beach."

"You mean," Bell looked at Kane with a frown, "you think someone will come today?" he asked skeptically.

"No. No, no, no, quite the opposite," Kane said, shaking his head. "No one is coming for us, Bell. Understand this. No one. If we stay here, we die here. We would have to learn to call this beach in front of us, and the jungle behind us, home. Until it kills us. And eventually – trust me – it *will* kill us. We're nearly out of coconuts, and much as we planned for rain, none has come. We need to move. We *need* water."

"But where would you go? What good will that do us? Surely we can find water nearby and stay. We're just two unarmed men, completely out of our element. We'll end up getting imprisoned – or killed! – by some hostile group. Or animals. Or anything… We talked about this yesterday and nothing has changed, has it? Just goes round in circles, like you said," Bell said despondently, his arms still binding his waist.

"No, it doesn't," Kane shook his head, smirking. "I have a plan."

"Oh good, a plan," said Bell quietly, clearly unconvinced, as he looked away to the ocean ahead of them.

"Aye, a plan," Kane was irritated by the man's lack of confidence in him. "Listen now man, listen. Obviously we are not going to walk to English Honduras. I am not a fool, regardless of what you seem to think. What we will do, however, is find the wreck."

"The wreck?" Bell's attention was again on Kane. "You mean find what's left of the Vigil? Why would we do that?"

"Do you see a ship out there searching for us?" Kane pointed out to sea. "Exactly. The English will never find us here. I am not convinced they even *want* to find us. We can easily be replaced with other men, and it would be easier and less time consuming for two more men to come to Honduras then to spend days, maybe weeks finding us. However," Kane paused, adjusting his position to sit a little taller. He saw he had Bell's full attention. "The Vigil was carrying materials from Jamaica, and god knows where else before it sank. We were merely a few passengers on a commercial ship, Bell. The precious cargo was not us, but *that*. And if I know our Empire, they will do what they can to keep from losing that cargo if they can help it. Whatever it may be. *So,* my thinking is, when those in Honduras realize the Vigil is not coming, maybe it sunk, they'll think, or perhaps it's only lost, they will dispatch a salvage crew to find and save the cargo. After all, it's far easier to find a destroyed sea vessel than two little men on some godforsaken beach. In short, we find said wreck, flag down said rescue crew, and," Kane clapped his hands in front of Bell's face, "we survive!"

Kane stood back to see Bell's reaction. Bell, however, stood rooted to the spot, unflinching.

"I'm not sure," he said finally, and Kane's confidence in having convinced Bell tumbled like a stone off a cliff.

"What do you mean you're not sure? Don't you —

don't you *understand?*" Kane snapped. Much as he wanted to remain calm, his temper quickly seeped through his cheery disposition. "The only other option, Bell, is that we stay, and make this beach our home! Until we—"

"Die. You've already said that. And I understand. But do *you* understand that we have no idea where we are? Say we were to leave, which direction would we go? We have no way of knowing which direction we were swept that night, right or left, north or south. So, what do we do? Gamble?"

Kane sighed. It was true. It was the very ingredient that made this decision so bitterly difficult to make. In his mind, it was the *only* decision left. The rest seemed almost straightforward, almost simple in comparison. He looked out to the ocean, it's deep blue glistened lightly in the sun. A warm breeze blew in from the waters and Kane stood and walked out through the soft sand toward the short, rolling waves. Bell watched him go, and then followed behind him.

As they left the cover of the shade, the intensity of the sun began to scorch its rays into their skin, though it was still only morning. The sand, too, was hot on the soles of their feet, but swiftly cooled as they reached the damp, hard sand next to the water. Kane reached the water first and stopped to feel the waves, also warmed by the sun, wash against his feet.

Bell came seconds later and stood next to him, looking left and right at their tiny, tropical bay. To their left lay a steep hill, completely covered with large bushy trees that resembled a head of unkempt, curly green hair, and a sharp face of hard brown rock that plunged down into the sea. Opposite it, to their right, the jungle ran flat to the water, where the trees sputtered and drown in the sea, submerged by the waves in a mangrove. Beyond it lay another hill, only just visible. The ends of the bay gave at once the appearance of protection and yet entrapment.

"I could be wrong… but I swear the current ran south that night," said Kane. "And, I found you walking north."

Bell said nothing and the two men stood with the water running over their feet and into the beach before reversing, dragging against them as it pulled back out to the sea.

"I have no idea which way the water ran," Bell finally said, staring intensely at the waves. Kane could see the man was racking his brain, trying to fish for a thought that could not be caught.

"It's going to take everything we have to survive this, but we *will* survive. Just not here. The way I see it, we have everything to gain by leaving, and everything to lose by staying."

"You plan to leave today, then?" Bell asked flatly.

"Not just today, but right now. For all we know the wreck could lie just a day away. Our journey could be over by tomorrow."

Bell turned and looked back at the beach, towards the network of dead brown palm leaves they had woven together with much difficulty and frustration only days before, in hopes to create a roof for a rain that had yet to show. The man sighed and turned back to Kane.

"Best start packing, then," Bell said, and began to walk, splashing, back to their shelter.

Kane smiled at the joke. They had virtually no belongings, and what they did have was already 'packed' inside each of their makeshift waistcoat slings. They had tied the sleeves of their tattered waistcoats they had worn the night of the wreck into shoulder straps, fashioning satchels out of them. The few belongings they still had were all that they had managed to grab on board before they found themselves in that vicious, dark water, being flung against razor-sharp rocks and gasping for air.

Before leaving, they split some coconuts against a sharp rock and drank the sweet, warm water inside. After thoroughly cracking them, they tore out and ate their fill of the flavorful white meat inside. Coconuts were one of the few things they had in abundance on this beach, so they packed more along for their trek.

Each man slung his satchel over his shoulder and walked along the beach, heading north. They trod the length of the beach, through hot sand and sun, until nothing lay ahead but thick, bushy jungle. To their right, waves lapped against the staggering rock cliff that plummeted into the ocean. Here, at the end of the beach that had been their home these last few days, both men stopped. Ahead stood low-lying palms, large trees with oval-shaped leaves, as well as twisted branches, vines and all sorts of thick bushes, forming a solid and natural border between the world of the jungle and the beach. First Bell, then Kane, looked back over the sand and towards the shelter they had built, which remained nothing now but an abandoned waste. Bell looked uneasily, with a gleam of melancholy in his eyes. Kane, however, analyzed the stinging hot sand and the bright, burning sun in the sky.

"We'll go through the jungle. We should stay near the coast, but not directly on it. This sun will only burn and dehydrate us." He thought a second longer, and added, "*and* we'll be more exposed, should Spaniards or the – damn it! – should any damned people that might live in this god damn place see us."

Bell cleared his throat a moment, ready to question this command, but Kane had already brushed aside a vine, ducked under a branch, and crossed into the wilds of the jungle.

III

The trek was rough from the start. The trail, if it could be called such, was laden with ferns and bushes, as well as small saplings that stood next to staggering behemoths of trees which looked as if they had seen the dawn of time. All of this vegetation was often clustered together so densely that it made walking impossible, and they would need to reroute far to the left or the right to be able to advance.

Was it more humid in the jungle, or were they just sweating profusely from the strain of walking so carefully through it, Kane wondered. All was darker in the shade and a slightly sinister feeling loomed there, deep within the forest. The leaves overhead were brightly illuminated by the harsh sun baking its rays into them. The ground was sandy at first, but the sand was quickly replaced by dirt as they walked further. As the ground grew darker, the mud began to stick to their feet with each step. One last reminder of the lashing rains that pounded that terrible night.

Bell had a poor pair of ratty, thin shoes, but Kane had nothing but his bare feet to walk on. This was something that was, to them, a fact of how they had survived the wreck and was never once discussed. Bell had just been lucky. Before now, Kane had not thought too much about this luck, but as he continually found himself stepping on sharp stones or being pricked or cut by thorny leaves and bushes as he navigated through this foreign land, he found himself hating the man for his good fortune.

The light sound of waves smashing against rock floated through the air to them, bringing with it the knowledge that they were not far from the coast. The wilderness between their last beach and what they hoped would be another one, however, was as deep and dense as Kane could imagine any section of this jungle could be.

Finally, sweating and panting from their trek that had turned sharply uphill and became very slippery, Kane spotted a place to stop. It was high on the hilltop, with a shaded yet clear, dry space where they could break and eat. They had not yet reached the coast and were likely only halfway there. They would need to pace themselves, he knew. Bell would say nothing unless he absolutely had to, in order to save face in front of Kane. It would have to be him who would call the break.

"Bell," Kane called, as he put his hand on the man's shoulder, "let's stop here. We'll have some coconut before we continue."

"Right. A break. Sure," Bell said, panting. Kane could see from the man's blotchy red face that he was grateful for the idea of a break.

They used Kane's rust-flecked pocketknife to stab holes through the eyes of a couple of their coconuts, drank the water and proceeded to smash the coconuts open over rocks, prying apart the hard, white meat with the knife piece by piece. It was the only tool Kane had that survived the wreck. Had he been working on that ship he'd have had his sailor's knife, but as a passenger all he had kept on his person was his pocket-knife. He never would have imagined he would need anything more.

Kane watched as Bell worked fastidiously to pull, piece by piece, the coconut meat out of its shell. He had large green eyes that, within them, held a certain inquisitiveness for life. They were similar to those of a child's, but in a fully-grown, young man's face. Within them was also an intelligent spark, and were they not covered by the anxiety and seriousness from their current situation, would have held quite a lively and playful gleam. Bell's face often held a look that revealed he was no stranger to pain and misfortune, yet at the same time was innocent enough to suggest he had not been fully affected by it. Yet, Kane thought. Not affected yet. He's still young, give him time.

With his long, wavy brown hair, his sharp jawline, his hollowed cheeks and his large, curious eyes, Kane thought Bell to be quite a good-looking man, and that he probably caught a fair bit of attention from the girls back home. He was tall, though not so tall as to stand out, but he had a lanky, thinner build to him. There was a slight awkwardness to the man as well, not unlike a puppy, and Kane wouldn't doubt for a moment that Bell did not realize his own advantages and instead focused on these more negative qualities, thus lowering his confidence.

In contrast to the youthfulness of his companion, Kane had a weathered face that made him look older than his years. It was the result, he knew, of too much sun and strain through his life. His hair was not pony-tail length, but at times hung down to his nose. It was brown as well, but with flecks of grey that flickered here and there in the sunshine. He was not a large man, but had broad shoulders and a solid frame. He was not fat, but neither did he have a lithe body either. He knew the gleam he once held in his eyes had long been extinguished. He'd been told for many years now that he had a hard, shrewd look to him. This look regained a hint of fire, of warmth, when he would crack a joke or momentarily forget his troubles, but he knew that once the fun was over his eyes would return to their cold gravity, like that of a hardened mountain man constantly pressed for survival.

"We we're close, were we not? To Honduras?" Bell asked suddenly, while still chewing on a piece. Kane nodded.

"Only a day or two away from port, they said." But as he saw Bell's face turn contemplative at these words, he added, "too far to walk though, I should think. We don't know how off course the storm took us. Our best chance is to find that miserable wreck. *That* I know we can survive." Of course he didn't know, but this he would never admit neither to Bell nor to himself.

Bell sat perched on a large rock, chewing, and looking as if he were turning over each word Kane had said, examining it from all angles.

"How do we know we weren't blow north of the wreck? In that case we won't find any wreck, but rather the port first. And if we *are* walking in the wrong direction of the wreck, it could be weeks or maybe months before we reach English land," Bell pondered apprehensively.

Months, Kane thought, and that was the last thing they needed to worry about now. Snakes, yes. Poisonous plants, yes. A savage's arrow, sure. But going the wrong way! The bastard! To bring up something like that.

"Finished?" Kane asked tersely and stood up, throwing away chunks of coconut shell but keeping the jagged bowl-shaped piece. He would add this to their collection of water containers for when the rains returned. The containers were built from young coconuts, which had only the top of the husks cracked open. After puncturing holes in the sides, they had tied strands from their shirts to create shoulder straps. It was not a perfect bottle, but they hoped it would retain most of the water during their travel.

They did not make it far down the hill from their lunch spot when Bell stuck up conversation again.

"Do you think any others survived, too?"

Jesus, Kane thought.

"You did, and so did I. Stands to reason others did, too, don't you think?" But the question did make Kane think. There were so many below deck when they first hit that rock. They thought they would hide from the storm, that it would be safer there. Poor bastards.

"You didn't have any family aboard, did you?" Bell asked solemnly. The man doesn't stop, Kane complained inwardly.

"No, no I was quite alone. Did you?"

"No, thank God. My wife wanted to come with me at first, but decided to stay in England after all. I can't imagine if... If she was aboard that night..." Bell looked saddened at his own mentioning of his wife.

Kane watched the man's emotions with a grimace. He grunted in reply, unsure of what else to say.

"I need to get to Honduras," Bell said with a determination in his eyes, "and send word I survived. I'm supposed to be sending money back to support her. I can't imagine putting her through the pain of thinking I'm dead."

Kane shot a curious look at Bell.

"You're a good man, still. Time hasn't corrupted you yet," he said, and stepped carefully over a fallen tree in the way. The slipperiness from the mud made the going very slow. One wrong step could find them hurtling down to a painful stop.

"I guess so. Maybe," said Bell. "Your family is back home then, too?"

Kane sighed. He continued silently a moment, and let his thoughts wander to all the cracks and crevices in his mind that held on to memories related to this question.

"Depends what you mean, I suppose. I have a father that I have not seen in years. My mother and brother... Well, they call the cemetery home now. So, not really, no."

Bell stopped, grabbing on to a thin tree for support on their way down the hill and looked at Kane, a wincing expression on his face.

"No wife? Or – or children?" he asked, which Kane returned with a fierce look.

"If I had, I would have mentioned them, wouldn't I? No, I never had any children. And my wife died long ago."

"Oh," was all Bell could say in reply, and he looked away, crestfallen. "Sorry I asked."

The men continued walking down and the land flattened rather suddenly and became immensely wet as the run off of the water down the hill had clearly collected there, making their feet sink a bit with each step. The sound of waves began to increase slowly, and a salty breeze of the ocean blew refreshingly into the stagnant air of the almost swamp-like rainforest they found themselves in. The shore was near now.

"It's okay," Kane shrugged. "It was long ago, now." Not that it makes it any better though, he thought, but it was his habitual response every time someone asked.

They continued to tread carefully towards the sound of the waves, each step slightly cautious before putting the full weight of its holder behind it. They almost constantly had bushes to part or plainly walk through, and their eyes scanned each bush, fallen leaf or branch for snakes, spiders or other hidden dangers. The noises and movements were constant too. Every dozen steps they would see something skitter or scramble out of the way, shaking dead leaves, or rustling bushes as it did.

Bell cleared his throat, and Kane knew another question was coming.

"How did – do you mind my asking how, how did she–" but Bell froze mid-sentence as Kane put his hand to his mouth and raised two fingers. Bell had heard it, too. A distinct, successive number of leaf crunches and twig snaps, similar to those they were making themselves.

Footsteps – somewhere nearby, maybe behind them, or perhaps to the left. They had just entered into a muddy gulch and as they ducked down, the branches they stood on oozed into the mud, slowly sinking. They hunched, eyes wide, darting at any signs of movement. Minute after minute they stooped as perfect statues, completely frozen.

Kane's mind raced at what could have made the noise. It was like a man's footsteps, but only one man, maybe two. Surely not more. Were they being followed? Was it Indians? Or some other people? It could not be Spaniards, he decided. They would not have ventured so far out from their station and if they did, they would be in force. The idea of there being more survivors a mere few feet away enticed his mind and for a moment Kane wanted to call out, but could not bring himself to take that risk.

Finally, Kane stood and Bell followed. There was not a single noise more. Perhaps it had been – well – anything. Kane took a step forward, his feet suction-cupping out of the mud.

Before he could take another step, however, an iguana sprang out in front of them, long and spiky, a mixture of green and tan. He barreled from a bush to their left over to a tree to their right, and proceeded to climb the tree. Branches rattled and one snapped, which came roaring down as it did.

"Could that have been all it was?" Bell asked softly. Kane snorted and let out a laugh. Bell laughed too and the tension from their situation seemed to melt away.

"Perhaps," said Kane, giving a smile as he watched the iguana climb, like a fluid, thorny ext-ension of the tree, lurching its way higher and higher.

"Funny. It almost... almost sounded like–"

"Aye." Kane cut him off before he could finish.

It was mid-afternoon, the sleepiest part of the day for life in these wilds. Yet all around them at irregular intervals, leaves cracked, twigs snapped, animals shook trees, birds sang, insects buzzed, and branches were torn and crashed down. The men stood, as children, new and exposed to this alien world that engulfed them.

IIII

The wreck was not at the next beach either. Not a single sign of their wrecked ship existed – not a shred of wood, a sail, a piece of cargo, nothing. There was nothing more than choppy waters, empty aside from some bits of reef protruding out of the waves. The beach too was only more sand with large pieces of rock, like sleeping grey monsters, in the midst of the golden sand.

"Shit," Kane muttered, wiping the sweat off his forehead.

Bell looked on intently, trying to see something that at a glance might not be seen. Some sort of clue that they were heading in the right direction, but found nothing.

"Do we keep going, then? Or go back and try the other way?" Bell asked, looking ahead where more jungle grew alongside the beach, until it wrapped its way around a bend, the rest out of sight. Behind was the bushy hill they had just climbed over. Neither wanted to go back.

"We go forward," Kane answered, watching the gentle bend in which the beach curved outward to the ocean. It was similar to the last bay they had found themselves in, only this one did not have a steep hill like the one they had spent most the day scaling and trekking through.

Directions were not difficult, they found. As long as they kept the water to their right, they could not fail. They would head north. The land next to the coast was easier hiking, too. It was less dense, though massive banyan trees dominated the land here, with their many strands of hardened vines forming part of their trunks. Each tree was immensely huge, like great elders of the jungle, and their roots snaked over and under the land, creating the main obstacle for the hike down the length of the coast.

While they had originally thought the vegetation near the coast dense, it was not nearly as full of foliage and life as the hill they had just crossed. They now moved quicker and with greater ease.

Strangely, however, this ease gave Kane some concern. At first he had been worried with what they may come across, or what may come across them in the wild. Now, however, his chief concern became his growing used to the dangers of jungle trekking and turning careless. Then trouble would surely strike.

They were half way down their newfound piece of coastline when Kane's stomach began to growl incessantly. His mind had been so occupied with other seemingly more important worries that he had not realized how hungry he had become. Almost immediately, he found himself bent on the idea of food – for *anything* edible to eat.

"It's getting darker," Bell observed, looking at the sky. Although deep, angry grey clouds had formed above, the dim light was from more than just the clouds. The sun was going down too.

"Damn it all, we need to eat before it's too late."

"Eat what? We hardly have any coconuts left. We ate too much on the hill."

"I don't know what! We'll have to find *something*, won't we?" Kane snapped. The coconuts were small and had hardly lasted a day between them. After a quick study of the palm trees, he decided, "I'm going further into the jungle. We won't find any coconuts here, I can't see a single one."

"I'll come with you," Bell decided, and though Kane thought the man could be more useful on the beach, he did not object.

Walking was far more difficult the further inland they went. All was green everywhere, overhead and, more importantly for Kane, underfoot. They continually had the idea that fruit hid just behind this tree, or maybe that one, but time and again they only found more leaves, branches, and the odd flower. Until Kane finally spotted it.

"Whoo!" Kane hollered and laughing he turned to Bell and slapped him on the back.

Ahead of them through the greenery was a long, bright red flower glistening like a beacon on a wide, soft leaved banana palm. Off the side of the palm hung what looked like at least fifty small bananas in a tight, circular bundle. They picked them each, still somewhat green near the stem, and ate a large number straightaway to satisfy their rumbling stomachs. They divided the rest to be eaten later. Both said little, but could not help feeling that Kane had stuck gold, and the resources to live a little while longer.

As the light of day subsided further, visibility became just strong enough to see the dark, hazy clouds rolling in from further up the coast. The first rumble of thunder sounded.

The roaring in the sky came as Kane had finished climbing a short palm tree, breaking the fuzzy yellow flowering bush that grew half way up. Out of the snapped stem flowed a steady stream of water from the tree, which Bell caught below in their coconut containers they had crafted days before.

Having finished filling the containers, the two men stopped and stared up at the dark, electric sky. Kane cursed and looked round at the trees. He thought of the roof they had constructed, whose only use had been to shade them from the hot sun. Now the rains would come and they were shelter-less – and they had neither enough time or light to build another now.

"Which looks like it provides the most cover to you?" Kane asked Bell, who stood watching the sky develop darker, more menacing clouds above them. Bell looked around in answer to the question.

"What?"

"The trees!"

"Of course! Of course… What about that one?"

Bell pointed at a tree with a massive trunk and hundreds of huge branches about a hundred feet to their left. Kane took measure of it and nodded. Bell was right, he thought, it seemed like their best option.

As they approached the tree, they could see the giant's trunk was half formed of large, dried vines as so many of the others around were, giving its base a hollow look. Towering above them, the twisting network of branches seemed strangled as each was wrapped and tied with many large circular leaves. Kane watched the dark branches for snakes, or God forbid, a cat, but he saw nothing but more branches. Bats flitted through the sky, some coming right up to their faces as they burst out of the hollows of the tree trunk, ready to hunt for insects.

I sure hope there's only bats up there, Kane thought uneasily as they pressed themselves against the trunk for the night.

As was typical at dusk, the howls of the monkeys sounded throughout the land, deep, and low and ominous. Tonight, however, perhaps due to the rain beginning to fall in fat, heavy drops, their howls were less angry and held more of a melancholic note. It reminded Kane of how a pack of dogs howled at the moon.

"It's warm at least, the rain. Not like England," said Bell, now concealed in black as the last of the light left the sky. His own mentioning of his homeland seemed to quiet him.

Normally, Kane would have left him in his silence. Tonight, however, he felt that conversation might distract him from his anxiety of the dark and the discomfort from the increasingly heavier falling rain, which dropped its way at random on his face and the back of his neck.

"What did you do in England?" he asked.

At first Bell said nothing. Perhaps he was surprised to be asked such a question from Kane, or perhaps he was lost in thought, regarding the times spent in his past employment.

"I worked in the stables," Bell answered as a silhouette.

"Stables?" Kane repeated, "It was a family trade, I'm guessing?"

"Exactly. My father worked in the stables and I took it up too. Natural, I suppose. Did some shoeing, cleaned harnesses, took the horses for exercise, mucked the stables… I was a good stableman, too."

"I know what a stableman does. So, what brought you to Honduras?" Kane felt himself thinking out loud.

"Lumber trade is picking up here, I'm sure you know. Can't fell trees in a jungle without horses involved and they pay a damn sight better than I received in London where I worked in a large stable. Little keeping my job there. Lots of other men ready to take my place. So," said Bell, adjusting his seating as a bitter tone crept into his voice, "I said goodbye to the wife and made my way to this wretched place."

Kane nodded, though Bell couldn't see.

"And the rest is history."

"History," Bell agreed.

"And that was the entire reason you came? Purely for the lumber industry, to make money and send it home?"

At this Bell was silent, then he sighed.

"Well, no… not exactly. I suppose I sought some freedom, to go overseas. To escape the stifling, dirty air of London. I regret it now, though."

"Well, should we make it out of here, I'm sure you will do fine at your work," Kane said, surprised with himself for complimenting his companion through this dire time they found themselves in.

"I'm not sure I want to work with horses anymore. Even if we do make it out," Bell said, his words laced with resentment.

"Oh," Kane replied little uncomfortably, unsure of what else to say.

"What did you do back in England, yourself? Kane is an Irish name, but you're from London, too."

"Well done!" Kane clapped his hands. "Brilliant ear you have there, picking up on your own accent like that. Aye, Irish name, but I was born and raised in London," and after a moment he added, "I'm sure you can relate."

"Couldn't have been easy," he heard Bell commiserate beside him.

"Aye… it wasn't. Could show you the scars from the God-blessed English if it were day light." Kane shifted uncomfortably. He did not intend to discuss his childhood pains as a consequence of his increased sociability.

"So, what did you do back home?" Bell asked, sensing Kane's stiffness towards the subject and so changed the conversation, much to Kane's relief.

"Home," said Kane, amused. "I haven't thought of London as home in ages... But, the docks, to answer your question. I worked largely on the ships moored in the docks. Wasn't just London, neither. Lived in many port towns over the last number of years, in this Empire on which the sun never sets."

Kane could hear Bell sit up straighter at this.

"Extraordinary! That sounds – just – incredible! Such an adventurous life you must live!"

"Aye, adventurous," Kane snorted. "And you don't think of this as an adventure?"

"Well," Bell was thrown by the idea, "yes, I mean, maybe it is an adventure. But it's surely not an enjoyable one."

"They aren't always... but, aye, I've had some adventures," said Kane as thoughts of past journeys began to flash in his imagination. He thought of strange lands, and stranger people when Bell interrupted.

"So, which ports have you lived in, then?"

"Ah, god, quite a number. Let me see if I can remember them all. There was Bermuda for a while, then Bombay in India, St. John's in Newfoundland, Kingston in Jamaica, and then Gibraltar."

"India and Gibraltar…" Of all the places Kane had listed, Bell made a point out of those two. They had struck a chord somewhere in his head. "Gibraltar… Say, did you ever hear of that English ship headed for Gibraltar from India? The one with all those women and children aboard?" The conversation fell silent, but not for long as Bell quickly continued, "I remember reading in the papers some time ago, in London, before leaving for this place. The Dartmoor it was called!" Still Kane said nothing. He shifted and cleared his throat, but otherwise remained silent. "Yes, the Dartmoor. Awful, awful business. It was off of some godforsaken island of the Canaries when they were attacked. Murderous degenerates. Nothing I hate more than murderers. Yes, the Dartmoor, you must have heard of it?"

Finally, Kane snapped.

"*Dartmouth,* not Dartmoor, Dart*mouth,*" he said, irritably. "Aye, I'd heard of it. I ought to have. I was on the damned thing."

Immediately Kane's throat tightened. Why did he say it? What in the hell did he wish to accomplish? Surely, it was nothing to boast about!

"You were…" Bell started but trailed off in shock. When he regained his words he exclaimed, "The *Dartmouth?* But I thought… But I swore… No – there were no survivors? I thought they all…" But Bell didn't finish his sentence. He couldn't.

"No, not everyone," Kane began, but paused a moment before continuing. "There were a few that survived that day. Very few. The papers were far from accurate in their reporting. When they discovered a few of us did survive they did not want to admit to their mistake. The title 'no survivors' was too dramatic and too bloody heart-wrenching to – to correct." Kane said with a quiet intensity that was simultaneously both frightening and sorrowful for Bell to listen to. Kane could have hit himself. He was not ready for the questions that would come pouring out of Bell now.

Bell, however, had none.

"Dear god," the man said. "Your wife, and… I'm sorry."

Kane said nothing in reply, unwilling to incite further conversation. The knot in his stomach slowly loosened, however, as nothing was further said.

It was far from silent, however, as they sat in the muddy forest floor. The countless heavy drops ripped through the leaves and fell down onto them as thunder rolled above with the rain. Each had his arms wrapped around his legs, as they sat exposed and defenseless to the wrath of the elements. And neither of them slept a minute.

HHH

"Since you have seen so much more of the world than I have, perhaps you know better," Bell began, as they made their way drearily back through the trees to the coastline the next morning. "What is it, if you know that is, that Spaniards do to their captured English?"

Kane sighed. Back to this, he thought. Back to the fear and incessant worry. He was worried enough himself without focusing on it. Without letting the fear grow larger with stories. Without letting it well up inside of him.

He remembered first seeing Bell on that next beach over from where he had washed up. That was when he had first made his way up the coast to find help as they now did again. He remembered how happy he had felt then, seeing him, after having been so lonely those first days on that beach. Being alone in this wilderness, with nothing but his thoughts and his fears was hell, and he had been overjoyed to have a companion to survive with.

Almost immediately, though, Bell had begun expressing his incessant worries. His never-ending fears of all that was near, or could be near, or maybe did not exist at all. Sometimes, with so little food, he thought the man's heart would give out from over use.

"Well," said Kane, clearing his throat. He felt as though he were walking through a fog of exhaustion from the complete lack of sleep the night before. "I've never been captured, personally. But… I suppose that the Spaniards are much like the English."

"What do you mean like the English?" Bell looked at Kane mid-step, his face jolted in shock. "Haven't you heard the stories? We're nothing alike!"

Kane smiled a little, enjoying the response.

"Oh, I should think so. Like the English were in America, or as they are in India or God-forsaken Africa… they, like us, are men who travel to far off lands in the name of God, country and a King. But God, to them, often has a silent 'L' and is far more yellow and material than a holy spirit in the sky. I mean gold, of course. The gold that they believe runs in endless supply in these lands. With their advanced weapons, military tactics handed down from the

Romans, and a black book called the 'Bible', they landed, broke existing empires and subjugated anyone they found." He saw Bell about to interject, but continued loudly over him, "*but*, empires are always spread too thin, and those seeking glory often find, I think, desperation and abandonment instead. Purely existing and holding any control trumps all else, I would say. So, to answer your question, I ask myself what would such desperate people do when they find two even more desperate Englishmen?"

Kane had not intended for such a monologue, but he felt his self-control lacking and his mind fuzzy with lack of sleep and food. Thank god for the bananas they had found yesterday, he thought, but as of this morning they too were gone.

"They would want us for profit, I suppose," Bell said, thoughtfully. "To find out about the wrecked ship. What it was carrying. It's location." Kane nodded. "Profit through torture?" Bell asked, to Kane's irritation.

"Sure, torture. If they are desperate enough. And cruel enough. They are men after all."

"Yes," Bell nodded, "but man is born good, remember. It's a lifetime of situations that make them evil." He seemed to reassure himself of this belief. "I don't like what you said about the Bible, either." The stableman added, flashing a sideways look of offence.

"Oh, come off it, you're no idiot, even if you speak like one," Kane cracked a wide smile. "Didn't take you for a Jesuit nor a monk, Bell." He was beginning to have the most fun he'd had in many days.

"I'm an Anglican," Bell retorted, to little effect on Kane.

"Ah! Sure you are! Sure you are. My mistake, my good man. And how long have you been one of those?" Kane mocked.

"You laugh, but God is with us here, even now. He will see us through this struggle. We have to have faith," Bell said seriously and assuredly, in contrast to Kane's fun.

"There's a change from all the talk of dying and the questions of torture, eh? Have you forgotten your religion 'till now?"

Bell blushed.

"I – I only said that in fear. I'm scared here, but I know, of course, that God will not abandon us. I still have my faith!"

"No, no, no," Kane shook his head. "What you still have is *life*. A beating heart and breathing lungs! This," he motioned around him, to the dense, green jungle surrounding them and the bright blue water within eyesight, "this is your god now! The jungle, the sea, the wild. It decides if you and I live or die now. If we have food and water, if a mighty and terrible storm comes and wipes us out, if a jaguar decides to bite and break your neck, if savages–" and at the word 'savage' Kane turned to something he heard moving to his left.

He was not sure what made him turn towards this sound. Surely there were many sounds all around them. This particular ruffling noise was slightly different, however, from the norm. It was there, through the bushes, the great leaves and the short trees that he saw it, if only for a moment. It was only a glance, but he locked his eyes on the dark, brown face of a boy, with his hair loose in his face, his bare chest displaying a small necklace of colorful feathers and a piece of sharp bone-jewelry jutting out of both sides of his nose. It happened so quickly, so unexpectedly, that he was still in full stride and had turned his gaze forward when he realized what he saw.

Kane's whole body turned on the spot, his head sunk into his neck and his back hunched over, ready. But nothing more was there. The boy had vanished, and without a noise! Or maybe he and Bell had made too much, he thought in panic, to hear the boy's.

"Savages what?" Bell asked angrily. "If you think you are going to tell me–"

"Sh-h! Bell, shut up!" Kane implored quietly.

"What the–" Bell started, ready for the argument, maybe even a fight should it come to that, but then he saw Kane hunched, with wide, terrified eyes and the color drained from his face. Kane motioned for him to duck and Bell did instantly. Kane made his way over, careful to make quiet steps and grabbed Bell's shoulder.

"What is it?" Bell whispered frantically, with eyes moving up and down, left and right, trying desperately to see what caused such fright in Kane's face.

"Saw a savage boy," Kane whispered.

"What! Here?" Now Bell, in turn, went pale. He looked to Kane as if for an immediate answer to this unexpectedly dire situation.

"Aye, here!" Kane hissed, so quiet he was nearly silent. A boy would not be alone, he thought with his mind racing. Surely there would be more! Or he would bring more if there were not.

He searched, as if trying to see through the trees and their thick, vine bound trunks, through the large ferns, the leafy plants that grew scattered, the vines that hung like a curtain at the theater, the arching, spiky bushes with their red, triangular flowers jutting out, the dense tropical bushes stemming sideways from the trees which hosted them.

Nothing. Even the wind died, leaving everything very, very still.

Leaves and branches began to shuffle madly to Kane's left, making his heart pound violently and his muscles tense throughout his body, but as quickly as it had begun the noises had stopped. They waited, eyes unbreakably fixed on the spot. It could have been an animal, Kane wanted to assume. But he knew it could have also been the boy scrambling away. With his senses heightened and adrenaline gushing through his system, his mind began to work at manic speed, processing entire streams of thoughts both consciously and subconsciously within mere seconds.

Where could the boy have gone? He didn't know which was worse, knowing the answer to that question, or not knowing. It was as if the Earth had opened up and swallowed that child!

Forget the Spaniards, he thought, what would *these* bastards do if they caught them? They may not know Spanish from English, but he and Bell were white men on their lands after all. Stories of men captured by these kinds of savages played swiftly in his mind, and his teeth began to chatter until he shut his jaw with one hand. Unlike white men, they would not care for profit. No, theirs were stories of revenge and pain. In regular times, he spoke with respect and fondness of the natives of these lands, but how quickly that changed when he felt his life teetered on the line.

"Bell," he whispered, the words barely coming out, "grab that stick by your feet." An idea had occurred to him, the only thing that might get them out of this nightmare.

"Why?" Bell asked.

"Just do it, god damn it! Grab the god damn stick and drape your coat over it." He did the same with a similar stick of similar size and shape near him, covering it with his own ripped waistcoat he typically used as a makeshift satchel. "Now, rest it against your shoulder, pointing up, like mine. We are going to stand up slowly and we are going to walk, head high, forward," Kane ordered, the very thought of this task frightening him to the core as he did. It did no less for Bell.

"Are you insane! You are going to–" Bell began to argue, visibly shaking, but Kane stood up.

He rested the draped stick against his shoulder like he had known men in the military to do with their rifles when they would march. The savages must outnumber them, he thought, not that he could see the bastards. But if they think us to have weapons, and that they may lose even one of them in a fight with us, perhaps that will be enough. Perhaps they won't attack. Or, he thought dreadfully, perhaps they would attack out of pure spite for the military.

Bell followed suit, trembling at the knees – they both were, but just hoped it would not be visible to the onlookers.

Bell began to retch, the nerves getting the best of his stomach, but with so little food in his stomach nothing came out. Kane grabbed him by the arm and pushed him in front of him.

"Walk, damn it! If you vomit you will do it walking!" he whispered with silent severity.

Kane's heart raced, yet his thoughts fell completely from his head. He did not know where they were going, or how far they would go, but they marched. It was a bluff, and an awfully bold one at that, but he thought nothing of it now. He simply put one foot in front of the other, not even bothering to brush the sweat soaked hair that hung in his eyes.

They marched like the military men they were not, with pounding hearts and wide, terrified eyes. Yet nothing came. No arrows, no poison darts, no screaming men with painted faces leaping out of the jungle with spears – nothing.

As they walked, a half hour or so later, sweat pouring from every pore, blinding them, Kane began to wonder if he had indeed seen the boy. He *had* mentioned savages as he saw the child. Could it have been a trick of the mind? They had barely slept for nearly a week now, were low on food and drinking water, bitten by more insects that he could count, and were constantly on edge – was it not possible he had imagined seeing the boy for that instant?

He shook his head. Was he really questioning his sanity, now? God knows, he thought, he *had* seen the boy. The image was far too real to have materialized so instantly in his mind.

He looked round at the greenery. He had meant what he said about the jungle being god in this place. He had an indescribable feeling that the jungle knew him, knew his pains and his sins, both his light in life and the abyss of darkness he carried. He was being tested, and if the jungle could not yet have his body, it would start with his sanity.

~~IIII~~ I

Kane stopped and looked up through an opening in the trees at the position of the sun. It now hung at its peak, streaking its rays of heat through the canopy, casting bright, green-filtered light down upon the two men. He knew from its position that around two hours had passed since the initial scare, but being conscious of every second and moment, those two hours had felt an eternity.

His hair and clothes were soaked through with sweat, completely saturated, and hung uncomfortably to his face and body. Kane could see that Bell looked just as miserable. He had wiped the sweat from his face and eyes so often with his dirt-stained hands that he now appeared to have a grotesque, streaky face of war-paint.

Not the humidity, nor the heat, nor their weariness slowed their pace, however, or their dogged determination to survive. While, since their shipwreck, Kane largely seemed as though fear were to him as civilization was to this strange land, completely contrary to one another, neither of the men were more afraid than the other. It was at this two-hour mark when Kane and Bell had stumbled upon a shaded, idyllic clearing in the trees. With this finding, in addition to there being no sign of any savage confronting them, that Kane decided to call for a break.

"We're good, Bell. We can stop here," he said, heaving a sigh. He took the stick that had acted as a prop would in a play out of its cloth cover. Kane planted the branch into the dirt and leaned against it, resting.

Bell looked once again, staring deeply into the wild around them, even up at the tree tops, as if one more check yielding no results would decide if it were safe or not. Kane could see the concern on Bell's face.

"If they wanted us dead or captive, they have had plenty of time. Let us rest a moment," Kane said as he closed his eyes a few moments.

Bell nodded, and threw his stick into the dirt beside him. And so they rested in this dry, open patch, with the blue sky above them, but still with plenty of shade. In this small, relatively comfortable space existed three wire-thin yet tall fruit trees. One had four bulbous orange fruits hanging from it which Kane knew to be papaya.

It felt to Kane as if the jungle had applauded their survival thus far, and had decided to reward them with this pleasant plot of land and a simple meal of its fruit. Ravenous and thirsty, they divided the fruits and ate them immediately. After they finished, they gathered the smaller, green, unripe ones for later. Unlike at home, nothing edible went wasted here.

The area they had found was not a clear, grassy knoll or valley like one might find in manicured Britain or other places in the world, but had low lying and easily trampled bushes, plants and tall grasses. In short, it was the closest thing they had found to a grassy knoll here in the jungle.

Here the immensely tall, broad reaching, umbrella-like trees surrounded them. Each draped like a shawl, with so many vines and leaves and plants leeching off their massive life force, that nearly none of the trunks were visible. Varying shades of bright green and black-green, where the sun did not touch, streaked through their space. There was no sign now of the rain that had given them such a blow the night before. Only light, delicate clouds floated in the otherwise harsh, hot blue sky.

Kane and Bell let themselves bake a while in this sun, drying the mud and muck they had sat in during the previous night, until dusty, light brown dirt fell from them in clumps. Feeling they were finally in some degree of safety, and being thoroughly exhausted, they napped in the warm shade.

An hour had passed when Bell finally turned to Kane.

"Ready?" He asked.

Kane looked at him, a little surprised. They had barely uttered any words the last two hours they had spent here. In those anxious hours they had, in an instant, become animals hunted. Their existence had been thrust into survival at the sight of one small boy, and though they needed rest for their bodies, their minds would not rest upon awakening. Having undergone such a frightful situation, Kane had expected more fear-stricken questions from Bell. Yet, if anything, the man looked momentarily resolute. A firmness sat deep in his eyes, where before Kane had only seen vulnerability and despair.

"Aye, good sir!" Kane replied in his taunting way, but as they grabbed their few possessions in their torn-clothing items, he could not help but steal a couple of short glances at the dirt-covered, sunburnt, lanky-legged man.

Strength was what he was wishing from the man for days now. Strength, like that which the men he had served with at sea used to have. Especially in *this* situation, strength was key to their success and endurance. Yet now that he saw the very quality he was looking for in Bell, he wondered – why did it make him so uneasy?

They began the next leg of their trek, but had hardly gained any ground before they came to a complete stop. The jungle had placed a swift-moving and formidable obstacle in their path.

"Damn it," muttered Kane despondently. "That's a good river."

He eyed up the divide from where they stood to the other side of the steady-moving, murky green water, which was made no doubt higher and faster after the last night's heavy rains. The jungle grew immovably thick next to the river, with trees leaning at an angle over the waterway and their vines hanging so low they nearly touched the moving water.

"How…" Bell trailed off as he eyed the water. The land on the other side lay at least fifty feet away from them. "I can't swim."

Kane said nothing. He could not either, but was glad Bell admitted it first. They went back and circled over slowly to the beach, as the bush was far too thick to walk right next to the river. There the river was far wider, but Kane believed it ought to be shallow enough to walk across. Even here the river emptied into the ocean at a quick pace. Kane admitted, though only to himself, that it was impossible to see the bottom through the muddy waters with the leaves floating waywardly on top.

"I'm going to try," Kane decided, eyeing what he believed to be the narrowest part of the river, although it still required walking blindly for far longer than he was comfortable with.

"But, what about crocodiles? Couldn't they be here? Anywhere?" Bell asked, eyeing the water that looked as if it swallowed anything from sight the moment it was under the surface. Kane clenched his teeth.

"Sure, there could be tens, *hundreds* of them in there, but do you have a better idea? Do you think this is a good time to try and learn to swim?" Plus, he thought, if there are crocodiles that hear us, you're in far more danger going in second.

Bell raised both his hands in capitulation and stepped back. Kane turned and with a few preparatory breaths began to cross. It was immediately deeper than he had expected, and stronger too. The water reached over his knees and tugged hard on his every step. And with every step he took he sunk deeper and deeper into the warm green-brown water, the ground soft and shifting under his feet. Soon the water was up to his chest, and Kane held his makeshift bag and the coconut water containers over his head. He was only perhaps a quarter of the way across, he realized, and the water still had yet to reveal its deepest point. To go further they would have to swim, Kane realized, but more likely would be swept out to sea and drown in the current if they tried. He turned around.

The two went back into the jungle and further up river, trying to find a narrowing. The river hardly narrowed, however they did manage to find a place where the span tapered perhaps ten feet. They chose to take their chances there. Insects buzzed and rattled on as they sat against a leaning tree by the water and contemplated their barrier in silence. Finally, Kane sat upright.

"We could make a rope with vines tied together and try and float across."

Bell blinked.

"Are you serious?"

Kane opened his mouth, but did not respond. It was not the reaction he had expected from the docile Bell.

"There is a hundred ways that could go wrong," Bell said, incredulously. "You would still need to try and swim. A rope won't just magically float you across. And even if you could, the rope could snag on anything in those waters and leave you in the middle to drown. No, it's a terrible idea," Bell decided.

"Then I ask you again, do you have a better idea? Call it a terrible idea, but I hear nothing out of you!" Kane snapped, thrusting an angry hand at Bell.

"I'm thinking," Bell said, staying clear-headed alongside Kane's hot irritation. "Just let me think."

They sat against the tree on the edge of the sharp drop into the river. Kane stared at the water, racking his brain for ideas. Bell, however, looked thoughtfully at the tree next to them.

"We fell a tree," Bell said with a solid sureness in his voice. He was convinced he had found the answer.

Kane smiled, glancing up at the great tree. It's roots and trunk looked as sturdy as anything he had ever laid eyes on.

"And how do you want to do it? Hm? Pull hard on the count to three?"

"No," Bell laughed at Kane's suggestion, and then said with a grin, "no, of course not. We'll do it with my hatchet."

Kane stopped and locked eyes with Bell, frozen. He was rigid as a steel rod, unable to move.

"What hatchet?" Kane finally asked. Bell frowned as he saw Kane's reaction.

"I just told you, *my* hatchet," and after a moment added, "is that an issue?"

Kane, realizing how he must look, relaxed his face

and did his best to repress the icy shock that came with this revelation.

"Of course not, course not," he said, straightening his back. "I just… never realized you had a hatchet this entire time."

Like hell it wasn't an issue, he thought. You weasel shit, you hid it the whole time. A tool, yes, but more importantly a weapon. You hid a weapon from *me* this whole damn time! And you only produced it after you could think of no other option. Why hide a weapon, unless… unless you planned on using it at some point?

"I never thought we needed it, was all," Bell replied coolly, scanning the riverside to pick a proper tree to fell. "And we haven't needed it 'till now. We always had your knife to cut fruit or anything we need. A hatchet isn't much good but to cut small branches, anyways."

It's good for more than that, you bastard, Kane thought. It ought to do to split a skull, for example. His cold shock melted into smoldering anger, but he swallowed and tried his best to bottle it. The man outgunned him, now, and he would not lose his temper. He would not give him a reason. Not yet.

"Did you bring it for the lumber trade, then?" Kane asked, also looking for a tree in his anger.

"Exactly. I lost my axe, and all the rest of my tools

during the wreck, but I had my hatchet on me at the time and used it to cut free a barrel that was tied. I think, otherwise, I surely should have drowned. Looks like it's come in use once again," he said, turning back to Kane. Bell scanned Kane's face for a moment, gave him a confused look, as if Kane wore three faces at once. Then he smiled, seeing through Kane's façade of tranquility.

"Ay, come now!" said Bell, giving Kane a slap on the back. "It's nothing major! The blade got so rusted in the sea, the thing hardly cuts anymore I would bet."

Kane checked himself, and gave his best smirk that he could muster.

"Of course, of course. It's no problem, really," he said with unruffled passivity. "Glad we have another tool with us. Everything counts."

There was, perhaps, some honesty in Bell's story. It was, however, the *way* it was said that troubled him. Once again, Kane thought, since their scare with the savages, and even more so now, Bell acted with that strange sudden confidence. Or, maybe – perhaps it was that... Kane's thoughts scrambled in his head, unable to pair a start with a finish, all were loose ends as he watched the stableman's green eyes search down the riverside.

Something simply wasn't right, was all Kane could

think. Was it seeing my fears of the savages that brought on this change? Or, was it that in that moment he had conquered his own fears and cut off his suffocating anxiety, like a rotten branch from a tree? But no, the hatchet – the weapon he had decided to suddenly show... No. No. This he had all along. All along, from the first day he saw this man's sorry, salted rags on that godforsaken beach. But now this indifference, this – well, in short this… confidence?

Kane's thoughts twisted and jumbled again, and could not make sense of this suddenly baffling puzzle. Whatever it was, he decided again, something simply wasn't right.

Kane was filled with resentment that Bell's idea, at least so far, was the stronger of the two. As much as the man practically berated him for his idea, he had to admit Bell's sounded far less likely to drown either of them.

It did not take long to find a suitable tree that both could agree on. They were at the narrowest point in the river that they could see, and the tree in question was thin enough to allow the least impediment to being felled. Most importantly, though, it seemed tall enough to reach the other side and leaned midway out over the murky green water. It had a single trunk that split far above into twelve scraggly yet solid branches.

"Right then," Kane began, reaching his hand out to Bell, "if you don't mind, I'll do the honors, less you feel like working overnight." He eyed the trunk of the tree, hand still outstretched, deciding how best to begin.

"Don't trouble yourself," Bell said with a flick of his hand. "Just save your energy for when it comes down. Still a long crawl to the other side."

Kane, a dose of anger washing over him as his eyes bore into the back of Bell's head, stifled his response. He resolved to lean back against the neighboring tree and watch the stable boy embarrass himself in his attempt. He would look on as the act came crashing down, instead of the tree.

Again, however, he was heavily disappointed. Bell proved quite skillful with the rusted blade that was supposedly of little use. He worked his way, slow but methodically, back and forth along the trunk. Chipped wood flew as he sharply hacked into the tree's base. Kane recognized, a half hour later, that he likely could not have used the blade so efficiently, when a loud *crack!* echoed through forest. This was followed by almost as loud a groan as the tree gave up its desperate hold on the riverbank. It fell slower than Kane had imagined, like an incoming giant to the peaceful landscape of the other side of the river. The tree ripped through branches on that side of the water and with a thunderous *boom* the tree's canopy slammed into the ground. Now over the river, Kane and Bell saw the tree had not been as tall or the river as narrow as they had presumed. Nevertheless, the plan was working.

Bell, as victor with his river crossing strategy, proceeded to go across first. He wasted no time in undertaking this task. Hugging the fallen tree, face forward, he began, one arm at a time, to crawl his way very, very slowly over the quick moving river.

Kane fastened his makeshift bag and coconut water containers around his waist and followed, awkwardly lying down on the slick tree to begin his crossing. He reached ahead, without the true ability to see what he was grasping, and with one hand pulled while the opposite leg pushed. He was painfully aware that the tree was still wet from the night before, and in more than one section he began to slide off to one side. With a muffled shout of panic and his upper hand wildly clawing at any bark or plant it could reach, he would right himself again.

The fear of falling into this rushing flow of water beneath him surged icy grease through his veins and cold sweat dripped from his mouth and chin. He tried not to think of the possibility of a crocodile below him. With his head pressed to the tree and only seeing what was straight ahead, anything could have been lying underneath at any moment. He fought to not think of such a river monster leaping up with powerful jaws and hundreds of teeth to rip him off the log bridge and bring him to a thrashing, watery doom. He had scanned the river prior to crossing to quell this very fear, but there the thought stood, unmoving.

At long last Kane came to the bushy leaves of the scraggly branches that had formed the tree canopy. Once across and with his feet back on solid ground, his heart beating madly in his chest, he saw how feeble the bridge they had just relied so heavily on really was. The full weight of the tree rested on two branches that had dug their way, only just, into the riverbank. He looked at Bell, who nodded and scratched his cheek. The young man's lively green eyes fixed on those two branches as well, and were wide with concern, yet relief. With the added weight of both of them on the log, everything could have turned for the worse those moments ago.

Kane eyed the other side of the river they had departed from and scanned the trees again from this better vantage point. Again, he saw no sign of the Indians that had so horrified him. He still could not shake the thought of them appearing at any moment, regardless of his feigned confidence that they were safe.

"Bell," he deliberated aloud, "you know, I say we ought to do something with the tree. We won't be going back, and there's no need to create a bridge for others." To this Bell gave a small smirk.

"So those pesky savages don't crawl across, too? You're right, might as well play it safe," Bell said, and descended on the two branches that supported the bridge in the riverbank.

Kane watched as the man worked, hacking at the first branch. He pondered what Bell had just said to him. And the way he said it. Did he insinuate that the savage boy didn't really exist? That he had purely made the boy up? Concocted him out of thin air? That his repressed fears had got the better of him, and none of it was true? He wanted to raise the latent slight to the man, bring it to the light, but he thought better of it. He did not need to lose face over this affront, real or not.

Bell finished with the first branch, cutting clean through, but the tree remained still, and nothing happened. Only a few hacks into the second branch, however, and the tree groaned once again. Bell leapt back, hatchet in hand as the branch thunderously snapped, flinging leaves into the air. The trunk dug a scar into the riverbank as it slid aggressively into the river. At first it laid where it fell, the end of the newly constructed and now demolished bridge simply sunk its top into the river a mere few feet from the edge. After a few moments though, the felled tree shifted, breaking free of whatever ensnared it underwater, and, dragging the other side with it the tree made its way down river until it was lodged in the middle, water running around or over it, unreachable from either side. Kane nodded at the wrecked bridge.

"Ought to do it," said Kane, and Bell looked with a smile at the murky river.

"Must think yourself a real prize if you think a savage tribe will *swim* after you in that water. I think that boy back there got a good look of you and thought it just wasn't worth the trouble."

Kane shoved him on the shoulder and laughed and Bell laughed too, and they began their arduous trek back to the coast. Their only guide in this foreign land.

~~IIII~~ II

The pair had not gained much ground before darkness began to set in. Their walk, so far in to the jungle and with the vegetation so densely crowded, made for slow, anxious footsteps towards the coast. Not unlike the buildings and people in the metropolis that was London, Kane thought, so too did the plants seem to clamber for space, fighting and jostling both upwards and outwards for a glimpse of the sun, of some fresh air.

While the path was as slow on this side of the river as on the other, and the fears of snakes and other such terrible creatures ran deep in both Kane and Bell's thoughts, the overabundance of life did have its advantages for those who braved it.

The last drops of water in their coconut containers were finished earlier that morning, leaving their throats parched with growing desperation. They did not stay desperate long, however, as the two came upon a massive, tight grouping of bamboo. The stalks alongside the steep bank of the river shot up and arched outward in every direction, from the river to the jungle. It resembled an overgrown and wild head of hair, each stalk thicker than two of their fists clenched together, and at least twenty feet high. Kane recognized it from the other side of the river, though at the time he had paid little attention, being focused on more pressing matters at that time.

Kane took the hatchet from Bell this time, as he claimed expertise in this area over the man. First, he knocked on different sections of the stalks, and, where he found the deepest answers to his knocks, scraped back some of the fibrous casings before he hacked, with one short and swift stroke, into the exposed area. At first nothing happened, but before Bell could muster a smirk, Kane placed the coconut container below the cut, and with the jerking withdrawal of the axe a stream of water poured out of the plant and splashed onto the coconut. Kane immediately tried to angle and maneuver the container to catch as much liquid as possible, and with each subsequent cut he became better and better at catching the miniature waterfalls until all the containers were again filled, and they had drunk their share with blissful greed.

Kane left the bamboo plants behind with a feeling

of regained confidence and usefulness over his partner. This proved somewhat short-lived, however, as when they came nearer to the shore, Bell had cut down a handful of coconut trees with skill and aim so they fell in the least dense area of the forest, where the coconuts could be gathered with ease.

The day's adventures had proved itself taxing on the pair, and after a lengthy amount of time, the coast and the calm ocean waters of the ocean gradually came into sight. Kane began to take notice, as the ground vegetation became sparser and walking became once again easier, how slow they had in fact been moving.

Though full or satiated were poor words to describe how Kane's stomach felt, he admitted the fat of the coconut had taken the edge off his hunger for the time being. The growling beast inside had settled.

Returning once again to the ocean was bittersweet for Kane. While he was comforted to see the ocean and its vastness, he could not help but feel a pang in his heart as he looked across the river. So much effort and time was spent on such a very small distance. What if there was another river like this, or one even larger, right around the corner? He tried to force such thoughts out of his head before they crushed him completely.

Both Kane and Bell agreed to construct a simple

lean-to shelter that night, regardless of how pleasant the few wispy clouds in the sky appeared. Chopping a triangular wedge into a thick-stumped tree along the beach, they hoisted the end of a nearby fallen branch into this frame. They gathered a mixture of dead, dried palm leaves and laid them along the branch as a roof for their natural tent.

As the day came to a close, like the slow shutting of a door, the divided world of the rustling, crashing water and the land, lush with life, became slowly and almost unnoticeably dimmer. Kane lay next to Bell, propped up on his arms with his elbows in the sandy dirt, facing the water. Kane was struck by a sudden reminiscence for a small home comfort he would often partake in around this time.

"Know what I miss?" Kane grumbled, his voice rough as they had hardly spoken in hours.

"A bed? Maybe a feather pillow?" asked Bell, while uncomfortably shifting in the ground, trying to relax but doing a poor job of it. Kane smiled.

"Why, ground just needs a bit of molding is all, just bunch it together and voila! You're feather pillow. No, Prince, I miss ale!" Just saying the words made him gulp a little, wishing for the acidic hoppy taste on his tongue, the light warming of his stomach as it washed down. Bell chuckled.

"Ale? I haven't thought much of it – at all, really.

Now you mention it though, it would be nice," considered Bell. Kane grunted in agreement.

"Aye, ale. A nice strong ale, just to put all this on a slightly duller, rounder plane. Or rum. Hell, wine would even suit me right about now. When the barkeep asks me, 'What'll ye have?' I'll answer 'Anything, my good sir! Just make it blur my vision a little." Kane said the last words quieter, trailing off as if they were just for him.

Bell looked back at the water from having stared at Kane amusedly.

"Civilization," he then muttered, nodding, "I wonder what the first conquerors here, vile men that they were, thought when they drank their coffees and spirits in the new world. So unlike anything else around."

At this Kane snapped out of his alcohol-filled daydream of times past, and looked directly at Bell. A flash of entertainment crossed his eyes.

"Civilization? Started this way, though, didn't it? Man deriving something from nature," he motioned with his eyes and his head to suggest the wild around them, as his hands would have knocked off a leaf had he used them. "Even the great city of London was once just a gathering of trees on a river."

"Sure," Bell said, a little apprehensively. He felt he was getting roped into another of Kane's opinions.

"But even the alcohol you mentioned is a sign of our civilization."

Kane shook his head and raised a finger.

"No, no, see your wrong, you contemporary. You think that because you see the genteel, the refined and mannered aristocrats of our day sipping fine liqueurs, that this is a sign of sophistication and must be 'new'. But spirits, ale, and wine and all of that has been around thousands of years. Thousands. We've added a few names and such, but we're no more advanced than those 'barbarians' of the day. *Or* those savages we saw today, for that matter."

"That *you* saw," Bell said, immediately, with a hint of frustration. "Okay, if spirits existed a while, what does it matter? I would rather live in such times as modern civilization than back with the Romans and barbarians."

"Ah the Romans. And we are so much greater than they, because they had, what, slaves? Yet the Americans and us rely on the same source of labor. And the children of the poor who are forced to work in the workhouses, in daily hells, aren't they also living a slave-like existence? The only different I see between us and the Romans is that we built larger, better ships that could bring us new lands to destroy. But remember that Britannia was once a Roman colony, and Caesar landed on our shore much like

Columbus washed upon these poor bastards' land," Kane said, and he eyed the hatchet as he saw flashes of annoyance from Bell as he finished. Reach for it, he thought, and I'll bring my knife on you so fast you will meet your God faster than you could have thought imaginable.

Bell said nothing in response, and they both watched the inky horizon as bats began to flit their way through the indigo light. Bell felt the leaf-roof of their shelter.

"Glad we made *something*, tonight," he said. "We have too many nights like last night and I'm afraid our feet will rot."

"Aye," Kane nodded. "The jungle taught us a lesson last night. Not worth the extra small ground gained for no shelter. Need to make wise decisions, here. A wrong step and the jungle will strike us down like we swat a fly."

Bell looked at Kane with disdain as he said this. His brow furrowed.

"I've had enough of listening to you talk like this."

"Like what?" Kane asked, somewhat surprised. He had not meant to start anything, but the man was starting to smoke like kindling before his eyes. He glanced at the hatchet again.

"Like all this horror, this jungle we're surrounded in, is your God. You want to live in sacrilege, fine.

But, after being stuck under a tree in a thunderstorm, frightened for hours about savages in the woods, barely crossing a river and being eaten alive by insects while we still cannot find any remains of our cursed ship, you might try to not speak of this godforsaken hell as if it were a supreme being, or all-seeing, or – or–"

"God?" Kane suggested.

"–Yes, godlike," Bell said, with no less frustration at Kane stealing his thunder. "All this nonsense about Romans, and slaves – what does that matter here? We need to survive, not contemplate history!"

Kane sat silent, watching the man vent. Survival, he thought. And were you thinking of our survival when you hid our best tool these last few days?

Two groups of monkeys in the distance began to sound a chorus of drowning howls through the multi-leveled orchestras of insects, as if in reply to the shouting under the makeshift shelter.

"You truly hate this land, don't you?" Kane said suddenly to Bell, turning on his side to face the man.

"You're serious? Of course I do!" Bell said with a start. "I'd like nothing better than to watch it all burn. Well – no, that's not true. To watch it all be cleared. Chopped. One damned tree at a time, and then I would look upon the wasteland as retribution for putting me through this. For killing all those people on the ship and trying to kill me."

The sun was dying, and Kane shifted uncomfortably as he realized the hatchet between them would soon be swallowed up in the blackness.

"You think your God so great, or so I hear you confess time and again. Yet you blame this land that saved you and gave you an opportunity to restore your former life, when otherwise you would surely have drowned. Perhaps your God put you here for a reason?"

"I don't believe so," Bell shook his head, "The Devil tried to kill us like it did the others, and God intercepted, giving us this chance. All this, we're in the Devil's land now. There is no divinity to this awful place. But if I could dispose of it, and make way for a civilized world–"

And a small fortune for yourself, Kane thought bitterly.

"–I would do it tomorrow. So, to answer your question; yes, I hate it. And don't tell me, for some reason God only knows, you don't?" Bell asked, his words cutting and terse. At this, Kane thought a moment.

"I don't. No, I don't hate it. There is something here that calls me. I can feel it, sometimes, or hear it. No system, no set of laws set about by corrupt men in a building by a river. It's a clean slate here, isn't it? It's a second chance. Doesn't matter what the 'real' world holds for us, or what we did in it. It's like going to Catholic confession, but one you know is true." Bell was silent to this, though Kane knew he had thrown more sparks on the kindling, and Kane continued. "I'll make it to port. I don't want to die. But I do not like being reminded, daily, of everything I detest. Of the papers shoving their manipulative interests in my face. Of those men in the public houses and taverns, so easily influenced and controlled. Them speaking of those interests, blindly spreading their messages."

The sun had set, now, hundreds of miles to the west of them, casting a soft glow over the water from the fading light. Waves made their way into the shore in hypnotic fashion from as far as the eye could see. Clouds lay strewn across the sky like the billowing masts of a fleet of ships in mid-sail over a sea of pastel indigo. The trees and branches around them looked like foreground silhouettes with the muted sky as the background on a painter's canvas. Thin clouds above, invisible before, subtly caught aflame before the sky was completely extinguished.

"Do you ever think mankind was not meant to have come as far as we have?" Kane asked. "That nature, or God, or whatever you want to call it, made a mistake? And maybe the world would have been better for it," he said whimsically, sitting back from watching the last of the dying light and stared instead at the darkness above him in their shelter.

"You're mad. You're completely insane. I'm in the middle of nowhere with a madman. Just my luck," Bell said, as if to himself as much as he did to Kane. "You're like those lunatics that stand up in Hyde Park, or some bloody street corner, raving on about the system, touting some unsubstantial claims of conspiracy. Like it or not, it's how England, and the civilized world, works. And money and gold – they are King. It makes the world go round. You need money in this world, or have you forgotten that, growing up poor? Don't try and tell me you didn't, or you would not have been a dockhand, and you would not be here right now, trying to get to some god-forsaken little port in this hot, humid, disease-ridden middle of nowhere. So I've had enough. I've just had enough of this. You want to live with the monkeys? There's some calling to you now. Go on!"

Bell waved his hand, as if brushing off a fly, and with this gesture Kane felt a sudden urge to break those fingers off. With each word he felt degrees added to the heat of his blood. He reminded himself, however, that Bell was young, and with this thought he let the anger wash over him, over his shoulders and down his back.

"I've been you. Aye, I've been you, in a past life.

Got everything figured out, got a plan like a beach full of crab holes. Point is, it's a perfect damn beach, you say, when the sand covers the holes from view, 'till someone comes stomping their way through, and all the holes come out in plain view." Through the darkness he saw Bell roll his head to one side at this analogy. "I don't expect you to believe me or even understand me, but, damn it, listen anyways. I've got no one else here and much as I would prefer to talk to the monkeys–"

"Then please do," muttered Bell

"–they might just understand me even less than you will. Money – money isn't everything. Growing up poor or not, I've been around money. And, surprise, it neither made me or any of the others who got it any happier. It traps you. It's like a big hunt that everyone takes part in for a prison of gold walls. I've been where you are before, I've–"

"Then what changed you, hm? What made you the all-knowing fool you are today?" Bell snapped, but though the words were chosen to maim, the anger was not there anymore. He was too sleepy from the day and his words became mumbled and drowsy. Kane thought for a moment before proceeding.

"Made some mistakes. One in particular. Well, perhaps two in particular. The kinds that make you take a hard look at yourself, at the direction your heading. Makes you realize the world is not a story-book. There are no heroes and villains. We're all both every day. So, I decided to play the villain no more, and to for once try and be the hero of my own story, impossible as it might seem," Kane said thoughtfully and with such dark insightfulness that he lost himself in his memories and had not noticed Bell's snores straight away.

He looked over at the man, just a vague outline, a silhouette in front of a shadow, and sighed. He stared out through the shelter opening, at further shades of black. As he closed his eyes, he felt a chill creep into his heart. It did not enter him, for he knew it was already there, laying low in the background. He felt it there, in the empty black chasm that lay beneath his own perfect beach, lightly covered with sand. His chest tightened as he tried to sleep, and he felt the darkness slowly crush him as he thought of her face.

~~IIII~~ III

That night the darkness, like an extension of Kane's surroundings, leeched into his dream.

Kane felt his face. It seemed so real. He rubbed the tip of his forefinger against his thumb. There was a graininess of dust and more was falling, lightly like snow from above.

As he tried to squint his blurry eyes upward, he saw that not all was dark after all. Uneven, thin streaks of light trickled through the falling snow, casting visible lines downwards. The air was stale, warm and damp. A familiar smell, a sharp and horrible odor, clung to the stagnant air, unwilling to leave. Somewhere a rat squealed and skittered away.

The dust, which at first was only lightly irritating, now began to itch and tickle the back of his throat. He felt a sudden and unshakable urge to cough, and yet knew he had to quell this natural bodily function. It was not safe – and he understood the blanket of fear that rested heavily on his shoulders, on his neck.

A cough escaped, but it was not from him, it came to his right. He squinted and shadows began to form in this dark, bleary world. More and more materialized, until he realized he was surrounded – and they were all afraid. He could tell by their hunched stances, as if their posture would create less noise. Their eyes, reflected by the streaks of light pouring down from the floorboards above, were all fixed upwards with an intensity matched only by those whose life hangs on the balance of a thread.

An abrupt *crack* sounded overhead, and all the shadows instantly crouched lower. A child somewhere let out a frightened cry, and an instant later was muffled. The wooden boards of the ship that surrounded them creaked and groaned.

Now he heard shouting and screaming above, and the falling white and grey snow turned to a dripping rain of red. Movement above cast moving darkness down below. The heat intensified as a pungent, burning smell of newly created ash and charcoal began to fill the shadowy world. Orange-red flickers lit an area in front of Kane, and shadows began to scurry away from where it was brightest.

The urge to cough strengthened, rising up inside him, until he could take no more and began to hack into the crease of his arm. He instantly swung his eyes up and saw to his horror the movement increasing above.

He was not sure which came first, the immediate flood of glaring white light, or the screams. They seemed simultaneous.

The next morning Kane sat with his arms wrapped around his knees on the beach in front of the shelter where Bell still slept. He watched the sun which they never saw set now rise up in front of him. He watched the waves roll in and pull away, just as dreams that came so swiftly during sleep, yet so easily slipped away upon waking.

It was not a particularly wavy piece of coast, but the waves there twirled and tumbled on the rough, pockmarked reef that lined the beach within his sight. Leaves, black palm branches and a few pieces of driftwood lightly littered the otherwise unspoiled beach, leaving pure, bright golden sand to run in lazy curves along the coast until it collided with a towering, overgrown point nearby to the left that jutted into the ocean like a shrub-covered dagger.

He watched the sunrise. Sparkling slices of silver shone over the ocean as the black of the sky was dyed indigo and navy. The rippling water then shimmered as if thousands of diamonds lay just beneath the surface. As the sun rose behind the clouds on the horizon, faint hues of orange and yellow rippled off of the waves and painted the clouds, like stained glass in a church. The sun finally burned through the cloud, spreading daylight throughout the sky and the land. The day had begun.

As this spectacle died away, Kane found himself lost in events past and present. Some long ago, some happy, but all too soon his thoughts found a way to his recent past, survival, and the man that he seemed cursed to share this journey with. After his sleep, which his mind drank like barren soil drinks a much-needed rain, his thoughts were both clearer and yet muddier than ever. They began with strength and focus, but span in circles and often ran themselves into the beach, where the water would carry them out with the tide, into the depths where he could see no further.

Kane felt small bites on his ankles at first, which grew stronger and more painful the longer he stayed on the beach, watching the sun retake its throne in the sky from its nightly absence. Feeling they were biting into his self-made wounds from scratching, he retreated back to the shelter where Bell slept with his arm out of the palm leaf tent. He lay with his face half pressed into a mound of dirt.

Kane set himself down with his back against the nearest palm tree, and watched the man sleep. He thought once again about how to approach his new-found situation, but the more he thought the more layered and complex those thoughts became.

When had he been planning on using the hatchet? This was the main concern that kept swirling its way into Kane's mind, and he held a private crowd of debaters on the subject. Why had he not used it previously to construct any shelters, nor had he brought it out yesterday, even when an attack by savages seemed imminent? Only when he decided the best way to cross the river was by cutting a tree did he reveal the rabbit in the hat. So *when*, Bell? *When* were you planning on using it?

To say he had underestimated the man was a gross understatement. For him not to have brought it out before this point either meant that he had not truly believed Kane had seen a savage in the first place, or that he was just plain stupid and so fearful that he had forgotten about the only weapon he possessed.

No, Kane shook his head at this thought. No, you've had too many times with your life on the line to know that in such a situation you do not forget about any possible advantage you may have. And Bell had proven that same day that he was not an idiot, much as Kane had thought him to be.

So, *when* were you planning on using the blade,

Bell? Perhaps, Kane thought uncomfortably, Bell had been exploiting him since the beginning. After all, even when he had been a fearful shell of a man, he kept the hatchet, like an ace in his back pocket. Perhaps he had been using him, as Kane thought he might use Bell. And when Kane's usefulness proved spent, or if he crossed the line, he might find himself waking to a blade in the back. He did not want to believe Bell would be so deceitful and treacherous, but surely, he had been nothing else so far.

He would have to keep himself in check, Kane decided. Although his stomach grumbled, and his mood often soured, he would need to play another game – a game Bell had played from the beginning. A game Kane had not known existed. He crept too close to the line last night, and saw the anger that lay, like a beast, in the man's chest. There was no use surviving the wild, only to die at the hands of his companion.

Just then Bell stirred, gently at first, before hastily pulling himself from his dirt-pillow, scrubbing the dirt off his face and cursing at an ant that had found its way there to bite him on the cheek. He looked up with bleary eyes at Kane resting against the palm trunk, half groggy and half angry at his rude awakening. Kane gave him a wide smile, especially after seeing the swelling dot on the man's cheek from the bite.

"Morning, sunshine!" he boomed.

The scent first rode on the light breeze that drifted in to break the stagnant, midday air. As the two men trekked, Kane caught the slightest hint of which he had perceived at first to be nothing and kept on. The bright light of the day trickled from the tops of the giant trees down to the lowly, compact bushes around the men. The humidity was heavy in the air, and the pair welcomed the breeze to cool their sticky, sweat-drenched skin. As the next breeze rolled in, however, Kane knew the stench was real. It was as unmistakable as anything he had ever heard, seen or smelt.

He became too well acquainted with this smell in recent years, and he braced himself for what they would undoubtedly find. To say it was a vile stench would be to trivialize the awful, appalling power that it had on the senses. Finally, as it became impossible to ignore, Bell turned to face Kane.

"What the devil is that smell? Something rotting?"

"Aye," Kane nodded, "*something's* rotting alright. Not too far now, I'm afraid." He said, with reservation in his voice.

The smell continued to grow unbearably as they

advanced through the jungle near the coast's tree line. It was only moments before Kane found the source of the reeking odor. There, through the trees at the edge of the beach, lay the bodies. Bell moved closer, drawn like a magnet, while Kane quietly tried to entreat him to move on, past the corpses. The man continued, however, toward the dead in a stupor. Kane followed.

The scene was every bit as gruesome and terrifying as Kane could have feared. He could not count the bodies that were strewn where the trees met with the beach. Not because there were too many to count, but because they littered the beach in pieces. A torn arm lay nearest to him, fingers outstretched as if frozen in an attempt to survive, though detached from its shoulder. One corpse was torn in half at the waist, with the victim's head lying near its feet. Kane wondered what the creature would have thought of their body being disposed in such a way. Maybe, he thought, they wouldn't have cared. Surely it paled in comparison to the brutality of their death.

They must have died the night of the wreck, Kane assumed, though few appeared to have drown. Sharks had torn these unfortunate souls, or their bodies anyway, to shreds. Jagged bite marks had dug out one corpse's side and another's belly, leaving gaping holes in both, but no entrails. They had already been eaten.

Whether the gruesome corpses and their torn extremities belonged to men or women Kane could only guess. Only one was identifiable as a woman, but this was only due to the fact the body wore a stained, shredded dress, which the waves had raised to a disrespectful height.

The carcasses were discolored and covered in ugly, dulled blotches of purples, greens and blues. The grisly bodies and their scattered pieces looked like they had belonged to giants as they swelled to unnatural sizes from the bloating of their decomposition. They resembled grotesque balloons to Kane, and he would not have been surprised if one should completely collapse with a sharp prod. All were covered in black crawling ants, giving the corpses an eerie, quivering look. Four large black-winged vultures with shriveled black heads worked at ripping into the torn bodies with their beaks. Many of the exposed bones had no doubt been their doing. Oddly, there was no blood left at the scene, the ocean water having cleansed it days ago.

Kane stood at the edge of the beach, unflinching, piteously viewing the macabre sight. He knew too well that he and Bell could have easily suffered the same fate, but his mind would not be able to fully reflect on this until later. He had blocked out all thought, let alone contemplation.

Upon fully taking in the sight, Bell hurried away and started retching by a tree. With the smell, the sights and now the sounds of Bell, Kane immediately turned to vomit too. The little contents left in their stomach made this a difficult task, however, and soon they both walked further into the jungle, and stood watching the scene from a distance.

"We can't leave 'em. Not like this. It's not Christian," Bell said, his voice pouring with sympathy. The imploring in Bell's eyes spoke far more than his words did, and though it pained Kane profoundly, he shook his head.

"Like hell we can't," Kane said quietly, yet sternly. "We have no choice."

Bell looked at Kane as if he had suddenly grown horns out of his head and hooves for feet.

"How do we not have a choice? We have the choice of getting those scavengers off them. We have a choice of doing them a damned kindness, don't we?" he asked with a desperation and compassion that would have made Kane agree, had he not known better.

"Look. I would like nothing better than to bury these poor bastards," said Kane, glancing once more at the gory landscape. "But the fact is they are dead, and they are rotting. If we get a sickness in handling their rotting bodies, you'll wish on your God's name you saved yourself first and walked on… Horrible as it is. We're still alive and need to do what we can to keep on living."

Kane could see the internal war in Bell's eyes, between what he knew in his heart to be proper, and what he knew was necessary. With watery eyes Bell turned away and tore off further into the jungle.

"I hate this place," he said, with a quivering revulsion as he walked away. "I – I just… I hate it!"

Kane glanced once more at the carnage, and with a heavy heart and weak legs he left the unfortunate corpses behind.

~~IIII~~ IIII

The humidity worked as a slow boil in the bush. It was as if a small flame burned under a large pot, the water steadily and unnoticeably increasing in temperature until bubbles suddenly formed and the water took notice that it was, in fact, boiling.

The two men hiked on, sweat continuing to pour creeks and rivers from every pore. They perspired from their face, to the small of their backs, to their calves.

Kane had little time to contemplate Bell's strategies or games any further before his stomach united with his thoughts and turned him again on a ravenous path of finding food. Food was not usually so dire, as given enough time and distance they would normally find some kind of edible fruits. In these lush lands they often found enough, too, that they had the luxury of avoiding the plants that neither of them knew.

Today, however, was different. Many brokenhearted times they had passed fruit trees – papaya, mango, even passion fruit, with nothing left to harvest, the fruits being already picked or completely rotten.

The more the day went on, the more starved they became, and the hungrier they grew, the quicker tempers flared, turning the air to a noxious poison. Even the very noises that resonated from the depths of the jungle seemed altered, sounding deeper and more irritable, as if to reflect the men's desperate state.

After another coconut tree, yet again, left no crop for them to reap, Bell turned to Kane with a finger pointed in accusatory rage.

"We should have buried the bodies this morning! I knew it!" he seethed with gritted teeth. "Where are all the fruits? All these trees we've found, more than we had seen before, and with nothing left! We should've buried them this morning, but no! And now God has cast us out and the Devil has taken what little food we had and left us to starve!"

Kane's head felt gallingly hot at this point. It was as if he could feel his brain heavy and jarring in his skull. He looked at Bell with eyes narrowed in disgust, one twitching.

"You want to die of consumption? Eh? Is that

what you want? Find yourself pale and weak and coughing up blood? You imbecile, I've had enough of your shit for one day. Go back and leave the food we do find to me."

"It would have been a good deed. God wouldn't have punished us for burying them. But now look at us. Now we're punished for leaving them in that horrid state we found them. I shouldn't have been talked out of it by you!"

"Talked out of it by me? As if you could have buried them even if you wanted to. You weak, miserable shit. You were the one who vomited whatever food you did have, and made me vomit mine. If you had had a stronger stomach, we wouldn't be *so* god damn hungry!" Kane fumed "Imbecile!"

"At least I'm not stupid enough to think I could float across the river tied onto a vine!" Bell retorted with a blow that took Kane aback. "Maybe we should hunt or fish. Maybe that's the answer. Your precious jungle is obviously not providing anymore, so maybe it's time we took things into our own hands."

"Hunt? How would you propose we could possibly do that? Bow and arrow? Throwing my knife? Set traps? With what bait? Do you think things through before they come flying out of your mouth?"

"And fishing? Why couldn't we fish?"

Kane thought a moment. He was ready to rip

apart all of Bell's ideas, but this one had caught him.

"That's possible… maybe. But how do we cook it? We can't build a fire. If we want to avoid Spaniards and savages, then a beacon of smoke is not the way to do it."

"I don't care *how* we cook it, or if we cook it at all! I'll eat its eyes and tail at this point I'm so hungry!"

"We might spend all day trying to catch one just to fail," Kane considered. "And in that time, we're losing ground we could have gained."

"We need energy to gain ground! *Energy*, old man! Which comes from the food that we cannot find!" Bell ran his fingers through his hair in a frenzy. "And here's – here's another question, how do we know we're even going the right way? What if all this ground you want to gain is in the wrong direction? Maybe the wreck was in the opposite direction. Maybe the British sent a salvage boat all the way back there and further, and we're just going to die here miserable and starving in the world's wasteland," Bell piteously moaned. He looked like a man cracking at the foundation, tearing at the seams.

"I'll tell you why we're heading the right way," Kane said, his anger dissipating along with his spirit, being replaced instead by a weak sadness. "Those poor bastards back there with pieces of their bodies missing. That's how I know we are heading the right way."

With that, Kane took some heavy steps and slumped against a tree, his head in his hands. Bell watched broodingly as the man tried to summon any extra reserves of energy to carry on.

Kane sat alone a few minutes, his eyes closed to black out the world around him. He found little comfort in this, though, as his stomach's growling began to dominate his thoughts. Kane grappled with a weary and slipping mind to create some plan for food when Bell snapped his fingers. Looking up, he saw Bell holding a long, dead stalk of bamboo.

"Where the hell did you get that?"

"Further inland," Bell said, analyzing his find. "We passed a pile of them just back there."

Kane then watched, as if in a dream, as Bell went to work on transforming the bamboo. He set the end down on a relatively flat stone and fished out his hatchet. He lined the blade up with the bamboo's end and with a sharp swing split the end of the shaft. He rotated the bamboo and with another *crack!* split the end into four even pieces. Kane watched in astonishment as Bell then pulled on a vine hanging from a tree near him and hacked it until it came down. He spread the split ends of the bamboo apart with the hatchet and slipped the vine in between each piece of the stalk, so that each of the four ends bent out and away from the others. He finished by tying the remainder of the vine in a circle near the base of the split ends, strengthening them. He handed his brand-new spear to Kane.

"Use that knife of yours to sharpen the ends. I'll go to find somewhere to fish," Bell said, his dogged look of determination unwavering.

"*We'll* go find a place," Kane said, finally standing up. He'd be damned if Bell was going to do all the problem solving and give him orders. Kane mused on the idea of where best to catch a fish. "If we find a creek, we could dam it with rocks and funnel the fish to where we stand, ready with the spear."

Bell replied to this with a wave of his hand.

"That will take too long."

"What will take too long?" Kane asked, his words laced with insolence. Admittedly it was not a quick solution, but what else did they have?

"Every part of that. First, we would need to find the right size of creek, which could take days. *Then,* we would need to build the dam, which depending on the size of rocks we find could take hours or even a whole day alone. *Then,* we need to hope that fish will actually come. There would be no point to fishing if we're going to starve ourselves for another few days in hopes to catch a fish."

"That's what I was saying all along," Kane said,

his jaw clenched. But to this Bell waived his hand again.

"No. No, fishing is not the problem. The idea is the problem. Have you not seen the reef over there?" He pointed further down the coast from them. The beach was an oddity made of rocky black sand, the colors running from heavy greys to deep black where the waves swept the shore. The tide was out, and so the darker shades lay out near the sea. Though Kane had missed it, Bell was right — there were dark brown and black pieces of reef and rock protruding out of the waves. Quite a lot, too. The water of the bay was littered with them.

"You want to…" Kane trailed off, as Bell's plan became clear to him at once.

"We're going to stand above the ocean on those rocks and fish while the tide is still low," Bell said, smiling. He was evidently proud of his idea. "Fish might even be trapped in a pool out there, if the water is low enough."

"Okay," Kane nodded, "that's the plan, then. But" — he hesitated, and grudgingly said — "my feet will tear like thin paper out there. I don't have shoes."

"I have no issue doing it myself," Bell shrugged. "Just sharpen the points for me, so I'm not doing everything myself." He smirked as his words clearly barbed Kane, whose face reddened.

Kane opened his mouth to retaliate but Bell had already begun walking toward the exposed reef, their makeshift bags slung over each of his shoulders. Kane grabbed the coconut water containers and swallowed his words, along with some pride. He followed behind.

Kane rapidly sharpened the four points of the spear and handed the tool to Bell. As he gave up the spear, however, an entertaining thought struck him and Kane grinned at Bell. Bell took the spear, but upon seeing Kane's smile, one that was not without a hint of malice, he grew plainly uneasy. Bell examined him a few seconds longer, unsure of what to expect, but as Kane said nothing, he turned his back and made his way out to the ocean.

Kane watched with amusement as the young, lanky man went fully clothed and shoed into the water from the black sand beach. Near its lowest point, the tide hardly brought the water above Bell's knees. His long brown hair, stretching down his back, swung awkwardly as he tried to gain his footing on a rock that would allow him to stand above the surface. Kane watched as Bell hoisted himself up on the rock, but before he could fully stand, a strong wave knocked him, mid-stance, back into the water. Kane chuckled with delight as Bell wiped the water from his eyes and looked to see if his failure was noticed.

Kane waited until Bell finally gained a strong footing on a rock before he advanced into the jungle to try his luck for anything edible. Kane searched in a grid pattern. First, he would hike well into the jungle, scanning the wilderness around him as he went. He then would move about ten paces parallel to the beach, before doubling back to the coast. Each time he would return to the beach he would make sure to watch Bell, with great pleasure, as he struggled and wobbled over the reef. Even from the distance Kane could see the man was absolutely intent on spotting a fish through the glassy waves. He couldn't help but think how the Caribbean sun must be frying any of the young man's exposed skin, and wondered how much redder and more burnt he would later be.

As the time passed on, neither Kane nor Bell seemed to find any success with their fishing or gathering. Every fruit-bearing tree Kane found, even here, was picked. It was beyond frustrating. He watched the tree canopies for monkeys, or whatever could be picking all their fruit, but saw nothing.

Maybe half an hour after Bell had gone out over the ocean, the man exclaimed in excitement. Kane stopped in his tracks and made his way back to the tree line to watch Bell from the shade. Kane saw him far out on a reef, spear held high and poised. He stood still only a moment before he leapt forward, but slipped at the last moment and came crashing down with his knees on the sharp rock. Though he was a great distance away, Kane could clearly hear the stream of curses and shouts of pain as Bell picked himself up and washed his bloody knees with burning salt water.

Kane snickered at the scene, but only for a moment, as a thought suddenly took away his fun. He looked both ways down the dark beach and behind him, into the jungle. He kept his eyes peeled for the smallest sign of movement. As alone as he felt they were on the beach, he knew that at any time a face could reveal itself through the trees. He understood Bell's pain, but they still had to keep their discretion in these lands a priority.

After another couple of failed rounds to look for food, Kane saw the ocean water was starting to rise. Parts of reef still remained exposed over the water, but only maybe half that existed before. What bits that did linger over the surface were swallowed up every time a large enough swell rolled in. Seeing Bell in almost the exact same place, and with the same look of obstinate determination, Kane decided to call out to him.

"Bell. Bell!" Kane tried to get the man's attention while keeping the volume of his voice to a minimum. "We should keep moving. We can find another place to fish!"

Bell, however, paid no attention to Kane. Kane debated calling again, and louder, but felt sure that Bell had heard, yet ignored him. Instead the man continued his slow, wet walk in the heat over the ocean. He was walking on water, Kane mused, like Jesus himself.

It was then that Kane saw Bell visibly tense and jolt upright. He shuffled forward, making a few practice jabs with his spear, his body twitching like a cat during a hunt. Without a warning like he had done previously, Bell sprang forward, splashing into the water and plunging the spear swiftly downward. Bell was completely submerged and aside from some white foam, neither him nor his spear resurfaced. Kane bit his knuckles as the water rippled and broke against the surrounding rocks. Perhaps he missed again, and hit his head on the way down, Kane thought. Yet he saw no body. Kane took a few steps forward on the black beach in sudden anxiety.

A moment later, however, with a great burst of water thrown triumphantly in the air, Bell sprang from the sea. The first thing Kane saw was Bell's spear, held at the full extent of his arm, like Poseidon and his mighty trident. Impaled on the end of the spear by two of the four spikes, an open-mouthed silver and yellow fish writhed and struggled as it's life drained away. Its scales glittered and glistened in the sunlight, but paled compared to the brightness of Bell's face. Though he had salt water pouring down his eyes and nose, Bell was beaming from ear to ear.

Kane gave Bell a smile and even clapped his hands once as the man fumbled his way back to the beach with their meal on the end of his spear. You bastard, Kane thought at first, but then corrected himself. No, I suppose I'm the bastard, aren't I? As the waves touched his toes and Bell came flopping towards him, Kane could do little but admit to himself his defeat. Bell had become the provider and the savior. In what felt like overnight, he thought, I've become the incompetent one. The failure.

HH HH

Bell gagged as he forced a slice of raw fish down his throat. Kane laughed, watching him struggle to swallow the best cuts of flesh.

"Not eating eyeballs now, are you?" he teased. Bell shot him a look, but continued on to the next piece.

Kane had no issue with it himself. Sure, the fish meat was soft, rubbery, even chewy, but it had very little taste and no smell. Kane felt his stomach both welcomed the fish and was shaken by the first food other than fruit it had stored in several days.

The fish, from its tail to its mouth, was nearly the size of Kane's forearm. Kane had sharpened his knife on a wet stone and neatly skinned the fish, then sliced thin strips of meat from the head down to the tail that they now enjoyed raw.

"Wish we could have fire," a sunburnt, still wet Bell murmured.

He had taken off his shirt to dry, and the contrast from his milky white skin to the fiery red that the sun had dealt him looked severe and painful.

"You know we can't," Kane chewed another piece, "unless you want to write a personal account on being captured and tortured by enemies. In which case, please, be my guest."

Bell thoughtfully rolled a slice of fish in his fingers.

"Man isn't meant to exist without fire. It's our lifeblood. It warms us, cooks our food, mesmerizes us. It belongs solely to man. No other being other than man can create it, or even cares about it." Then he added, his green eyes darting a sideways glance towards Kane, "I wouldn't be surprised if one goes mad without it."

Kane stared at Bell with a hard face, thinking over the truths the man spouted. He picked up another slice of fish.

"No fire," he muttered, and ate his piece.

Later that evening, as the sun neared the horizon, the two men waded into the sea to wash themselves and their clothes. Kane smiled as he watched the sun-caked dirt and sweat form a cloud around him. The dirt slowly drifted away, freed from his body and able to return to the shore and the land once more.

He ducked into the warmth of the tropical water and closed his eyes as the waves lapped against his face. It was the most refreshing moment he had felt in weeks, and as he brought his head and whole body underwater his mind wandered back to his days at sea. The days when he used to sail, with the spray of a rogue wave flying up on to the deck and dousing his hair with water colder than this. Or the port towns, and all of the sights the sea used to bring him. But mostly, he thought of the freedom that the open ocean held. The freedom. Although, he considered as he came to surface again and looked bleary eyed at the shore, they were free here too. Just not in a place of their choosing. Or in a way of their choosing. So, was that really freedom?

He watched Bell as he worked the dirt off his skin mechanically. With the sun's lower position and the trees that lined the beach, a large section of the water was shaded, allowing Bell and his sunburnt skin to also enjoy a soak in the water. It was clear that having burnt his skin and later having had salt in his eyes from an unexpected wave put a dark cloud of sullenness in the man's disposition.

Kane lifted his arm to look at its wound as salt water ran off the cut. It continued to heal nicely, and though it looked as ugly and discolored as ever, he saw no signs of infection.

Kane smiled as he laid his head back in the water. He watched the clouds swirl in the blue sky as they grew dimmer every minute. He allowed his mind to wander back to the freedom of the ocean.

His train of thought did not take long to reach its terminal station, however, to that frightful night when the lightning crashed and the seas were not only spraying the crew on deck, but sweeping them off of it. Things could have been better, he thought, had he been running things. But he was only a passenger, and they steered straight into a reef. He had remembered seeing it as a sheet of lightning illuminated the blackness — that jagged silhouette breaking well through the surface. It was useless to try and bring that knowledge to the attention of the crew, as the wild winds and violent waters prevailed over all of them. It would have been too late, anyhow. He reckoned he was not the only one who saw it, perhaps even the helmsman knew, but what could he have done at that point? So they continued headlong into that bit of rock, which was nothing less than a resting giant that carved their ship in two. He remembered the sounds, the heart-wrenching *groans*, and *crunches*, and *snaps*. He had recognized it immediately for the retribution it was, even before he went overboard. Except he had not expected to survive. Not really.

As he dipped his head back underwater, Kane

couldn't help but remember being rocked over the edge of the ship as it came into contact with the rock. It flung him with otherworldly force and sent him plunging into the treacherous water. He had felt certain he would land on some of the rock that ruined their vessel, as did the screaming others that fell nearby. But, somehow, he narrowly missed it. It was only his right arm that had been cut open as he scrambled in the stormy water to make it up to the surface. A loose, splintered board of wood floated by and he remembered latching on to it desperately. He knew that despite the cuts and deep splinters that dug painfully into his hands, to let go was to die.

Another bright flash of lightning illuminated silhouettes of beach-lined trees and he kicked with all his strength in the direction of that far away shore. The lightning then died as soon as it had appeared, and all returned to darkness, confusion and fear. Fear of the sharks that could tear suddenly and mercilessly through him. Fear of currents that would drag him away from the shore and out to the open water. Even fear of other passengers, who could rip him off his splintered board to save their own life.

He soon lost the direction in which he was kicking, yet he kicked just as hard though his breath grew short and his legs burned. In such a situation there is no gun or knife to defend against anything.

All there was, all he had, was the ability to kick and push against the water as cold fear ran icily through his veins.

Finally, with one more flash he caught sight of the shore again. The wreck was now gone, somewhere far away. He thrust and struck at the water with every last bit of life he had, and put the entire focus of his mind and body and being into survival, regardless of how unlikely it had begun to seem. He swam for a time that could have ranged anywhere from two hours to two days, or anywhere in between. His head bobbed up and down in the water as he struggled to keep the sharp wood under his chest, until finally he kicked hard into sand. He remembered panicking at first, afraid there was something malicious beneath him, his feeling largely gone from his legs at that point. Soon, though, he kicked it again and again. All was black and he was completely blind as his lifeless, trembling legs first attempted to stand on the beach. He groped wildly, still holding the wood in case it was only a sand bar he had washed up on, but stumbling his way in an upward direction he found the tree line of the beach. A large wave from the storm water came from behind him and threw him down face-first, grinding him into the wet sand. Unable to stand again, he remembered how he crawled his way up the beach until the waves no longer touched him. Then, exhausted, with the rain still pouring heavily down on his back, he collapsed into blackness.

Kane stood up in the shallow water and looked toward the beach that lay near him now. The scene could not be more serene. Waves lolled into the shore and the palms and other thick leafy trees rustled their leaves. Wisps of clouds swirled lightly overhead, covering and uncovering the sun so that light was continually growing and lessening around them. Regardless of the calm that lay around him, the memories of that night proved too strong to ignore any longer and Kane moved back toward the beach, where the water was only ankle deep.

He sat down in that shallow water and watched Bell again. He seemed more relaxed than before. Kane remembered the first day he met him. It was not the first day after he awoke from that eventful and frightful night. That day he had mostly sat on the beach he had washed up on and waited. He waited for a sign, for some glimpse of salvation, of a single piece of the ship, a body – anything to come his way. Yet nothing had. When the panic and grief subsided, he tried to calculate where he was in relation to the wreck.

It came as a shock how nothing of the wreck lay in sight. He had expected to see something, but all that remained was his shred of the ship's deck that had saved his life. In the ocean, nothing existed but water. It was as if there never had been a ship, or passengers, and he just appeared here after a bad dream. It was his kicking he reasoned, or a current, or both, that pushed him so far away from the wreck and out there to that godforsaken beach he had washed up on.

He remembered the setting of that first day spent there on the beach, and how the following came and went much the same, completely isolated and alone. He had hardly moved those first few days, held in a trance and left deep in a state of shock. Having woken to such a radically different environment shook his grasp on reality. He questioned whether the beach was his afterlife and he had actually died that night, his body left to rot somewhere deep in the sea.

Fear alone stopped him from screaming and shouting for someone out there, someone who could hear him – anyone else who survived. It was the fear of being heard. He had been sure that the rest must have died. Surely all that he had heard that night was death and anguish around him. That was before he drifted too far away to hear anything other than the scream of the wind and the rushing of rain and rolling sea. There was no plan out there for anyone, no escape. There were only rocks and thrashing water.

He dragged himself up and out of the water and

walked back to the shade. Bell was already waiting there, his shirt and pants drying in what remained of the sun's heat.

It was on that first beach, after days of confusion, hunger and absolute loneliness that Kane had decided no one was coming. If he did not leave to find help and save himself yet again, no one would do it for him. Thus, he had hiked through his first jungle, over a small, dense hill that divided the coast from the next beach. And that was where he found Bell.

ⅢⅢ ⅢⅢ I

That evening, to their disappointment, their clothes retained some moisture from the ocean as they built their camp for the night. If, Kane thought, you could call their impromptu spartan shelter made of a single branch wedged into the crook of a tree and covered in palm leaves indeed a camp.

Rumbling and lightning flashes danced and stretched from the placid sea to the shadowy hills behind them. The daylight steadily decreased following the sinking sun.

"Good thing we built our camp in time," Kane observed, more to himself than to Bell, as the first patter of rain began to fall. Although the words were not overly important, he couldn't help but feel a pang of irritation as Bell made no remark or even facial response, but instead turned away. Kane waited a moment later and then erupted.

"Hello! Is anyone there? Of all people to have to

go through this with, I get a mute. A bloody mute. God, first he's nothing but stupid questions and now he doesn't talk!"

Bell stopped moving a moment, and Kane thought he might say something, but instead he just lay down with his saggy, damp shirt clinging to his back as he curled up against the inner edge of the leaf-roof.

"Look, I don't know why I'm wasting my time," Kane tried once more, "but there's only two of us here. I wish there were more, or I wish you were someone different, but there isn't and you're not. We need to speak to each other or we'll lose our minds out here."

Still Bell said nothing and showed no expression. Kane began to boil. Red-hot blood pulsed in his temples and his unexpected hatred for Bell escalated. How could the man be *so* insolent? Every thought surrounding Bell began to be filled with a dark and intense loathing until he was on the verge of shaking with rage.

"Speak, you son of a bitch!" Kane roared and felt any dignity he had slipping away again. Bell still sat motionless. Kane held himself, and tried to let the anger wash over him, but it lessened only slowly, like dripping syrup. His anger was irrational, he knew. But was it, really? In his ire nothing was clear.

He clenched his jaws, and tried to think back to

when he had first set eyes on Bell on the beach. He tried to think of how happy he had been then. He hoped it would calm him and save him a little face. Yet even through his anger Kane understood how little esteem Bell must still have for him. He shut his eyes and let his mind return to when he came down that hill after the trek from the first beach.

He had been solitary for days, he remembered. Stranded. Alone with nothing but his thoughts. It was a crueler prison than he had ever known. He recollected pacing up and down on that small, sandy beach, racked with self-loathing and despair. A few times he started walking out to the water, thinking he would finish what the wreck of the Vigil could not. He couldn't swim, so should he encounter a drop off in the sea he knew that would be the end for him. Yet, he always turned around when the water reached his waist and retreated to the safety of the trees.

At one point his mentality drastically changed and he considered building a permanent shelter for himself. He fancied putting the thought of life, life as he had known it that is, behind him. He did not want to return, then, to what had mentally tortured him so badly. He could learn to fish, to forage and to build fire. For a moment he had even lost the fear of his being discovered by a fire, he recalled. He might have stayed too, had he the right tools. But his simple rusty knife and his other trinkets would not prove much help, so instead he had decided to leave. No, he ruminated in the growing darkness of their shelter, he might as well be honest with himself, if no one else. It wasn't the tools that made him leave, but his thoughts. It was the need to find someone else to share his misery with. Someone to distract him from himself, that finally made him leave.

His first glimpse of this sorry man was undoubtedly the happiest moment he'd had since the wreck. Kane smiled as he thought of this. Bell had been hunched over in the shade near the beach, watching for any signs of movement in the water, just as Kane had been doing until that day. His face was as weary and frightened as Kane might expect a child's to be after having withstood those horrors. At seeing Kane, though, Bell's face transformed like an indecisive artist's canvas, from fear to disbelief and then to joy. They walked toward each other, laughing through tears and crying through laughter. Kane tried to maintain some form of composure, though his watery eyes made the mask paper-thin.

He remembered first seeing the man's sunburnt cheeks and ears, his spirited, youthful green eyes, and his long, unkempt, chestnut-brown head of hair. His clothing was shredded, it had suffered the same abuse as Kane's.

"Hello, old friend," Kane said to Bell. He had meant to say more but was too full of emotion to have the words come out.

"You don't know how good it is to see you," Bell replied, with feeling beyond his words.

Kane remembered how they embraced, so each could not see the other's tears of joy. He remembered how he had felt then and there, that they would surely survive.

Returning from his daydream, Kane looked at Bell, now just a stationary profile as the darkness and rain increased and began to pound on the shelter above. Drops of water fell through and onto his chest. My god, he thought. How things have changed.

That night, at times, the rain had turned to a full-fledged storm, battering their pathetic improvised shelter so hard that Kane was afraid the whole thing would blow away. Drops found their way through and turned into miniature waterfalls when the rain intensified.

The lightning edged its way through the sky, momentarily illuminating the jungle's subjects below. Deep, ground-shaking thunder would follow and all the howler monkeys within earshot would howl with as much power and awe-inspiring dread as they could muster.

The next morning, though the shelter held out

most of the rain, Kane still awoke to find his side lightly covered in mud. The mud was already beginning to dry and it suctioned as he pulled himself up and out of the shelter. It was an overcast day, almost reminiscent of England, Kane thought, if it weren't for the humidity and tropical wilds that surrounded him. It was by no means cold, not the cold he knew, but it was the coolest day yet.

What he would give for a fire right now, he thought miserably as he looked at the freshly drenched landscape. Though he argued with Bell about lighting a fire, he began to care less and less about the idea of being found by hostile forces. There's a chance they would not even be hostile, he thought, or even exist at all. It would be a gamble, but perhaps it might be worth it.

He cracked a coconut, and began his morning work of making breakfast, trying to get the pieces bite-size with the help of his knife. As he did this, he thought of the monkeys the night before. It was as if the monkeys thought the Great Monkey, god of all monkeys, had descended upon them to show His disciples what it *really* meant to howl. He thought of these monkeys, shouting and bellowing in response to the sky. Have humans really come so far in their religion? Kane thought of himself, how he had once been quite religious. As he did, he felt that familiar mix of regret and acceptance that one feels when they analyze certain areas of their past. Again, he considered how past actions and beliefs could return to strike you like an axe when you least expected it.

He glanced at the shelter. His movement had yet to wake Bell, or if it had the man did not show it. Speaking of axes, he thought sullenly, perhaps today will be the day, or tonight will be the night, that I'll find that hatchet dug square into my back.

His usefulness was deteriorating in this impossible situation, Kane mulled. Bell made the spear. Bell caught the fish. Though Kane skinned and prepared it he was all too aware that Bell's catching the fish was another point for Bell, and a point against Kane.

He took out the chipped and rusted knife from his pocket and scraped the blade against the ridges on his thumb. He could not kill him, he thought. Not yet. As much as he did not want to admit it the man was too useful at present. After all, he might be still stuck at that river and going crazy if it weren't for Bell. Though perhaps not, he thought. Perhaps he would have crafted another plan to get across. Regardless, the man he had originally found enveloped in fear and self-doubt had time and again proven his ingenuity and worth.

His mind brought him unwillingly back to the grisly scene of those unfortunate souls on the beach yesterday. He pictured being out there on that horrendous night, to have sharks biting and ripping pieces out of him as the others had, helpless and blind to defend themselves. The pure terror of it all… He shuddered. It was unimaginable.

Even his indication to Bell of the bodies being a sign they were heading in the right direction was not done without a motive of proving himself. It was based on very little, if any fact at all. Sure, the winds seemed to be consistent with that idea that particular day, but he knew full well the wind could have changed a hundred times over from the night of the wreck. He loathed that he felt it so necessary to prove himself, to *him* nonetheless. But this was not a typical situation. This was survival on all fronts.

He knew in his heart that they could be going the wrong way. It was a thought he fought to force out of his mind, but ever lurked in the background. Those bodies could have blown away further than they had from the wreck. They could be walking in the complete opposite direction. He had to retain some hope though, he thought, chewing on a wedge of coconut. Some glimmer of hope had to remain, or *all* would be lost. After all, he could be right, but he knew for that to be the case they would need to find more bodies along the way. Then he would be more assured.

Should they not, however, find those essential corpses… He looked at the shelter again, where Bell was beginning to stir. They would both die, he knew. But one sooner than the other. Much sooner.

~~HHI~~ ~~HHI~~ II

"Oh, what the hell?" Kane muttered an hour into their day's trek. He slowly shook his head.

Bell looked at Kane with a bit of a frown, then around at their lush surroundings and back to Kane.

"What is it?" He asked, confused.

"Don't you realize?" Kane grumbled. "Haven't you noticed? Look around!"

Bell did this once more.

"Notice what?" He asked slowly, with apprehension.

"The fruit!" Kane cried. "The fruit is gone! Again!"

Bell looked at the trees and with a startling realization saw Kane was right. They were next to two papaya trees and not a single fruit existed on them. Not even a solitary, unripe, small piece was left. The trees were barren.

"There's another one," Bell pointed out a banana

tree, with a handful of peels lying at the bottom of it. "What could it be? Monkeys? Savages?"

"Possibly," Kane glanced round himself warily. "These peels look like a human ate it. Don't know that a monkey would peel it in such fashion." He picked one peel and examined how it was peeled into three, neat pieces.

The men continued to walk, their eyes cautious for any movement.

"If that's the case, then it's a new type of warfare," said Bell. Kane looked at him puzzled.

"What do you mean?"

"Well, it's obvious," said Bell, with a gleam in his eye, "The savages have us surrounded and they've decided to kill us slowly, by picking all the fruit on our path."

Kane snorted and Bell grinned, but Kane could see the man's true feelings through his eyes. Although his mouth did it's best to hold up the charade, his eyes betrayed the smile. Out here... Kane wondered, anything was possible, wasn't it?

"What if it's insects eating the fruit?" Kane pondered aloud.

"Insects?" Bell scoffed. "Do you see any left on these trees? Why would insects peel those bananas? How does that make any sense?"

"Easy, lad," Kane said, not without a hint of

annoyance. "The insects might have already left, and these," he pointed to the two peels, "could have been left over, or already eaten before they came. Maybe… maybe they're on a path ahead of us."

"Do you even hear what you're saying, old man? You know, I'm curious," Bell remarked with a small smirk, but with a face serious enough, "with your doctrine of jungle religion, where do the insects fit in? I mean, you love all of everything that's here, right? The bodies, half-eaten yesterday on the beach, the bloody fact that we're continually on the verge of starving – everything, right? I suppose you even love the damned insects? Where do they fit in to the religion of one starved, crazy old man?"

"Look, Bell," Kane began, fully composed. He could see that hunger, or something, was starting to chip at the young man's reason and rationality, "when you start looking for fights like that, I'd love nothing more than to drive my knife straight into your mouth that's uttering these idiotic comments. But I won't." Kane did his best to speak evenly, calmly, and with poise. Even if his words were full of malice. "Let's settle on a deal, shall we? Let's be civil for a day and spend it in conversation. Only, one that's not full of moronic remarks and insults before you fall back into brooding silence, hm?"

Kane's last comment sparked something in Bell.

"Civil? You're going to talk to me about civility? Were you civil when you were screaming and cursing me last night? God, you're a hypocrite," Bell snapped.

Kane grit his teeth. There would be no peace. He regretted losing his temper and saying what he had the night before. Even if what he said was the truth, he should have held his tongue. What he would give for a friend now, as his mind began to deteriorate with the exhaustion of each day's hike, lack of food, and night after night of poor sleep.

"And as for your rhetoric rubbish… What do I care for your Romans, or your jungle God, or your Conquistadores, out here?" Bell muttered.

"The Conquistadores?" Kane could not help himself as the words tumbled out. "What do you care for the Spaniards out here? We are almost definitely on Spanish land, walking straight through it… Were you not shaking when I met you, thinking about the Spaniards? Trembling at the thought of their torture methods?"

"Okay," Bell conceded, and Kane believed he could see a little of Bell's old fear creep back in as he thought more of the Spanish. "Yes, I'm still afraid of running into… *others* out here. Yes, we need to keep our wits. I can hardly keep track of how many days it's been. If we find the wreck–"

Bell had continued talking, but just then Kane

stopped listening. He had heard a loud snap, somewhere ahead of them. A snap was nothing unusual. Movement in the jungle was as common as movement in central London. Branches fell and animals jumped or landed on the wild flora constantly. This, however, was an exceedingly loud snap. Something different, slower, with a heavier weight behind it than was commonly heard. Not that this was an overly scarce occurrence either, but it always created an apprehensive attention in him whenever it did happen. And there! He heard another one, and one more after it! His eyes traced the bushes and trees ahead of him for any movement, but the jungle was a veil as always, and he saw nothing. Kane heard it once more, further to the left, and he grabbed Bell by the sleeve. Bell looked at him with surprise and perplexity and saw a familiar anxiety start to build in Kane's eyes.

"What, savages...?" He said quietly, looking around him, but Kane tugged on his sleeve again. When Bell looked back at Kane, he saw he was holding a finger to his lips and eyeing the landscape carefully.

They watched, both of them. Sometimes in different directions, sometimes in the same. Nothing. Kane began to breathe more easily. Once again, he thought to himself, nerve-racking fear over nothing.

Always nothing. Well, better nothing than something, he thought to himself.

As Kane was about to divert his attention back from the wild to their path, however, a head shot up and ran – just visible through the vines and trees.

Kane's eyes bulged and his heart began to shudder, rather than beat. Before he could make up his mind on what to do, his legs made it for him. He found himself running at the man, his small knife out and ready, shouting and screaming. He was not used to moving so quickly through the jungle, but he narrowly shot left and right around the natural obstacles in his way, leaping over ferns, ducking under branches, racing around the great leafy trees. All the ground was still wet from the night's rains and he slipped and skid his way to where he felt certain he would find that man. Everything was a blur of green and brown and he felt ready to take on whoever was out there. He was ready for blood. He shouted an incoherent stream of curses and threats. With a mixture of adrenaline, fear and a shattering of his nerves, his war cry was completely unintelligible, yet utterly savage. He was a man unhinged.

And suddenly he wasn't. Rationality and con-sciousness gained a foothold in his psyche and he considered for the first time the possibility of being led into a trap. It could be the Spanish. It could be the

Indians. It could be a band of escaped slaves. And aside from one rustle that could have been any animal running away from the knife-wielding madman, there was no longer any sign of the head that had caught his eye back near the beach.

He slowed his run to a stop and not a moment too soon. A fluorescent yellow snake slithered down from the other side of a tree and in the way of what would have been Kane's path. Kane reeled backward and tripped over an exposed root, falling and splashing back-first into a puddle that lay next to the root. He continued shuffling backwards, head up and eyes fixed on the serpent. The snake stopped, seemed to consider him for a moment, tongue flicking, before slowly slithering it's four-foot length into the shroud of the wild.

Kane gulped and stood, shaken from his near fatal mistake. He looked round himself quickly to be assured that there were no other threats nearby, nothing visible anyways. He looked on in the direction he had been running. He had lost the man.

Shit, thought Kane, as he turned around. Where the hell am I? The sound of the surf seemed far away. It was now only a faint *whoosh* noise being actively buried under the shrill calls of birds, *ribbit*-ing of frogs, and the sporadic crunching of the living and mobile jungle. A slow, cold injection of terror and panic began to replace the hot adrenaline in his bloodstream as Kane's head darted left and right. He began to realize just how far he had gone.

As his heart slowed from the chase and the encounter with the snake, his physical sensation came rushing back. The damage he had caused to his feet became apparent immediately. He leaned against a tree, checking one foot at a time. Underneath the covering of mud he could see and more importantly *feel* the lacerations torn open from the many treks, as well as some new ones carved in from the chase. He plucked a few barbs and thorns that were dug well into his skin and he could see blood from the many cuts and scrapes. They were so plentiful and criss-crossing that they painfully reminded him of the many threads of cheesecloth. The blood began to mix with mud and drip brownish-red from his raised foot. He gently lowered his foot into the mud, well aware that with such bleeding he would need to clean and dry his feet sooner than later.

This thought, however, was of far less importance than finding his way back. He was sure of the direction he had come from in the last few seconds, but as he had weaved his way through and around the many obstacles in his way, he had no recollection of where to turn after that.

He felt as if the jungle, which constantly surrounded him, was now beginning to close in on him. The vines, the ferns, the trees, the shrubs, and the leaf-strangled branches inched closer with every breath. He swore the jungle was never as *wild* as it was now.

"Footprints." said Kane aloud. Yes, footprints! With the mud he could retrace his steps back, he thought with hope. He wasted no time and immediately began to follow his own tracks backward. He was slow and made each step gingerly, wincing as his mass transferred from one foot to the next.

It was not difficult to track at first. The mud was plenty, and the steps were deep enough to keep from being confused. He could see where he skidded and slipped here and had to pull his foot out of a small quagmire there. With his eyes darting ahead and back down again to the next track, Kane was covering a good amount of ground.

Only two minutes into his tracking, however, he came across a large puddle that he had splashed into on his way. The tracks vanished. A suffocating feeling of dread began to set in, again. In a panic he ran one way, looking for an obvious sign of a track, then back, then that way, then back. Soon, he realized to his horror, he was creating more and more tracks and the chances of finding the original ones were becoming increasingly thin.

He began to breathe heavily as he looked left, then right, then further right as fears flooded his mind. Fears of not finding the shore, of not making it back to the wreck in time. Fears of being lost to die out here in the density of the jungle. His fears and thoughts went further still and much to Kane's surprise, included Bell. He feared losing Bell, his only companion, forever. The very man that had been the subject of his darkest hatred, he found himself wishing intensely would be with him once more.

"Bell!" he called, but with a soft voice, anxious of who might hear. Within moments, however, this particular anxiety died away and he was shouting on the top of his lungs, "Bell! Bell! Where are you! Bell!"

He waited by the puddle, calling Bell's name sporadically, and with each shout felt the crushing weight of abandonment falling heavy on his shoulders. Soon he made up his mind to set out in what he hoped was the right direction. As he walked, fearful with each step that it was in the wrong direction, the torment of sudden and possibly lasting isolation built up within him, until he would shout "Bell!" again, and return to walking in silence.

It occurred to him, in his self-flagellating thoughts, that his moment of idiocy, his chasing what seemed now to have been a ghost, may well have cost him his life. There was no response from Bell, no sign or sound. While he believed he was walking perfectly straight, the noise of the surf scarcely seemed to grow louder.

He had begun to miserably debate how he would manage with no water or food. The water was back with Bell near the shore, and he only had his small knife to help him build a shelter for the upcoming nightfall. It was at that moment that from behind a massive tree trunk ahead of him stepped Bell.

"B-Bell!" Kane gasped, almost unbelieving of the sight.

"*Kane!* Keep it down!" Bell entreated him in a hushed voice. "Follow me… and if you see something go running just stay put!"

Kane smiled and chuckled a little to himself. He followed the man, surprising himself by thanking God he was lucky enough to be reunited again. It had been a long time since he had thanked God for anything, yet strangely he knew it felt right in this moment.

He followed Bell through a series of twists and turns that led back to the shore. Kane couldn't help seeing Bell in a different light now. He felt awash in relief and happiness at seeing the man. Maybe I've been too hard on him, he thought. After all, his insults could have only been defending himself. Perhaps I was in the wrong for taking it as an offence. Kane resolved to try and be more civil towards Bell and see how events would turn from there.

As they reached the coast, Kane dropped down on to the sand to tend to his torn feet. He plucked out a handful of thorns that had been stabbing and digging into his feet along the walk back to shore and proceeded to painfully wash them in the surf. He then tore off the sleeves from his waistcoat he had been using as a makeshift bag and bound a sleeve around each foot for protection. Lastly, he fastened the lining that remained from the coat to make a new, albeit less secure, shoulder strap.

"Thank you, Bell. Thank you. You have no idea how good it is to see you again. You have my gratitude for coming to get me," Kane said with a heartfelt sincerity.

"Save it," said Bell tersely, and looked down at Kane's feet. "Bravo, now your feet are damaged. Better hope that doesn't get infected. If you die from your own stupidity, don't think I'll be burying you. You'll be left like the others. What the *hell* were you running at back there?"

The reality of the situation had yet to occur to Kane until just that moment. While he felt pure joy and gratitude for finding Bell, believing he had come so close to being truly lost and separated, Bell was angry as ever with him. Kane now saw the bitterness and dark irritation that was plain on Bell's face. A cloud began to cover the clear skies of Kane's mood. What struck him next was the question itself.

"What was I running at?" Kane asked, bewildered. "The – the man of course!"

Bell's expression did not change. He did not even blink.

"The man," said Bell, not angrily but with disappointment. He cast his eyes downward for a moment before throwing them back at Kane. He spoke with a mixture of pity and unease, "the man, of course. What was it this time, Kane, another savage?"

"I don't… I don't know – do you mean to say you saw nothing of the man I chased?" Kane asked, still incredulous. His thoughts began to race with what Bell must be thinking of him.

Bell said nothing for a minute. A warm, salty breeze blew from the sea through the flapping leaves of the trees and tossed Kane's clumped hair in his face. As he brushed it aside, he saw Bell looking at him as if trying to read words in a language he did not understand. There was nothing friendly, or familiar about his look. Instead it resembled a look a stranger might give one whom he believed to be dangerous. Or mad, Kane thought bitterly. He's trying to assess how sane I am. Finally, Bell spoke.

"Kane, there was no man," he said hollowly, before adding, "just like there was no savage boy."

The words slapped Kane in the face. He felt a cold fury begin to build up. It tensed his neck, and he wanted to strangle the bastard for saying such an outrageous thing. Bell didn't stay long enough to see Kane's reaction played out, however. To Kane's irritation he turned and continued the trek. Bell walked slowly along the path that, what felt like hours ago, Kane had diverted from.

Clenching his jaw, standing and watching the man walk away, Kane latched on to his reason and knew arguing with him was futile. Bell had made up his mind about him and the more he spoke or acted against it would only further confirm to Bell what he had already decided was true. Nothing had changed, Kane knew. If anything, it had only worsened.

Wronged as he felt and as much as Kane would have preferred in that moment to turn and walk the other way, he submitted and followed Bell before the man left his sight. Nothing but a man with a hatchet stood in front of him, Kane reflected, as he hobbled after Bell. His reckless chase in the jungle had accomplished nothing. Nothing but speeding up that man's plans on using said hatchet.

~~IIII~~ ~~IIII~~ III

Kane eyed the sky through the old-growth canopy that hid them from the sun. It was dusk, he thought. Or hell, it must be dusk soon. It was not clear to say. The sky was not dark yet, though it felt like much time had passed. A grey and cloudy sky hung above, producing an even, white-grey light through the trees. Bright flashes from distant lightning fleetingly lit the sky, skewing the shade. Even the green was duller, not vibrant with life and color as usual, but dark and full of shadows.

Bell walked slightly ahead of Kane, as he had for the last few hours, only stopping on occasion to rest or have some water. The men strode alongside another coast, this one rocky, grey and wave battered. Bell seemed, to Kane, to have much on his mind. He would occasionally shoot a searching and concerned glance toward Kane, which Kane tried to meet with his own look of irritation and scorn. These glares affected no change in his companion, however. Bell would just slowly turn away, his face unchanged.

To hell with him, Kane thought. I won't be perturbed by a look. Nevertheless, he couldn't help but begin to lose himself in wondering what thoughts persisted in the man's mind. No, Kane reaffirmed, to hell with him. He would not let Bell get the upper hand. He would not let Bell be the one to decide on when the first death would come to their duo. He would not give him that luxury.

Overall, Kane admitted, Bell had not acted overly aggressive. There had been angry moments, but he had not wielded the hatchet as he might have expected. Bell clearly had no liking for him, Kane knew. The man seemed to think him quite useless, quite incapable of contributing to their survival. So then why didn't Bell end it? Much as Kane tried to stay awake late now, he always fell asleep first. It would be easy then. He would have no defense, so why not?

Then a thought struck Kane that had not before. Something obvious, something right in front of his face that he had been missing all this time in his growing paranoia. Bell was a *Christian!* A bloody man of religion! Of course, he wouldn't attack him defenseless, asleep, with his back turned. Not if he wanted to keep in the good books of the man upstairs! Kane scoffed aloud, incredulous that he had not thought of this sooner. It must be the grueling exercise, the lack of food or the exposure to the elements – or all of them together, for him not to have realized this until now! God, he thought, with heavy irony at his blaspheming choice of expression, that was why Bell was so cross these days – he was looking to provoke a fight!

Kane nodded to himself. That had to be it. The man surely saw no use for him at this point, regardless of his occasional feats. Bell had nothing but contempt for him and he sure as hell didn't engage him in conversation. So why keep him around, unless he was biding his time, waiting for the right time. Waiting for Kane to attack him or affront him in some way and Bell could find Christian solace in telling himself it was self-defense.

A second arrow of insight then plunged deep into his breast, spreading a chill to his heart. Bell's bag. Kane could see it, swinging from Bell's shoulder ahead of him as they strode carefully along his way. It was not a bag in the traditional sense, Kane corrected himself, but functioned as the closest thing that they could call a bag out here. What else was in his bag? What other danger resided inside that seemingly innocent cloth overcoat, with the arms strung together as a shoulder strap? After all, it was that bag that had housed the hatchet, concealing it for as long as it had been. Thank god I'm carrying the fishing spear, Kane thought. It gave him what little sense of security he had left.

What could it be? A pistol? The gunpowder would have become useless in the wetness of the storm. Unless, of course he had kept it in a tin container, Kane pondered. A dagger? That couldn't be much more menacing than a hatchet, but still. Perhaps it was some sort of poison? Kane brushed his fingers through his hair. This was possible, it would be easy to conceal. What if it was a map?

And at this idea Kane felt his train of thought divert to something equally disturbing. Were they heading in the right direction? And why, God, why weren't there more bodies? Bell couldn't have a map. *That* he would have revealed, wouldn't he? He had been walking, keeping his senses keen ever since their encounter with those that died in the shark attack, but nothing. Not a rotten thing was to be found but fruit. He had invested so much hope in those poor victims, that he should find more. It was the last straw keeping himself and his morale alive. But without more…

He thought of what he had said to Bell, days ago, about the Spaniards. Those seeking glory in the colonies often find desperation and abandonment instead. Purely existing trumps all else. Desperation and abandonment, he thought. I was more correct than I could have imagined.

Not all come for glory though, Kane reflected. He breathed deeply, as deep as he could go and breathed out as that unutterable shame came back at once. Some come to hide. Some come because they hope to God they can find a place where they know no one and can have a fresh start. Or, he contemplated, perhaps he ought to have just admitted defeat and sailed himself to Australia instead.

Kane travelled further back in his thoughts to when he had been young. How he craved adventure when he stared at those maps in the windows of those little English shops. How he stared at all the blank spaces, yet unknown. As he grew older, they began to fill in a little more each year. And each year, a little more, he felt his chance of adventure begin to slip away. How little he knew then of what real adventure meant, and how much of it he would come to experience.

But then, Kane thought bitterly, what the hell did he know then? He looked at Bell. What the hell did Bell know, at his age? To make him feel incompetent, a freeloader, a disgrace – incredible! He was gripped by a surge of strong emotion towards Bell, but none so intense as shame. He had such a profound feeling of shame for Bell that he was embarrassed for the man. Not that it made him feel any sympathy or lighten his outlook concerning him. If anything, he resented him all the more for it.

His thoughts returned to the bag, swaying in front of him on Bell's shoulder and a strong and sudden impulse to see what was inside of it arose in him. Soon it became difficult to think or see anything else. He resolved he would look that night, when it was dark and Bell was asleep. It would not be difficult. Bell slept so hard that he could practically destroy half their structure and the man would not notice. At least that's what he *thought*. Perhaps Bell stayed silent and only pretended to be asleep, the snake he was. He was surely treacherous enough that anything was possible. What are you hiding, Bell? Kane wanted to shout. What's in the bag? At this thought Bell turned around and squinted at Kane.

"What did you say?" Bell asked.

Kane blinked.

"What?"

"You just asked me something, what do you mean what?" Bell said, that strange look of concern and almost fear glazed his eyes. He looked at Kane as if he were a man with whom he had not spent the last — how many days? – together, but had only just met.

Kane looked away, his eyes wide. He could feel Bell's perplexed face piercing through him. Had he spoken out loud? He felt a discomfort like never before.

"Kane?" asked Bell, cautiously.

"I said nothing," Kane affirmed.

"Look, if you're planning something and you don't want to tell me, that's fine. I don't care. But don't tell me you didn't speak, that's just… well, that's just ludicrous." Bell looked at Kane uneasily. Yet as agitated as the man looked, Kane noticed, Bell was not afraid to confront him. He would not let this drop.

"Your bag," Kane said, at first wavering, but then followed with a more decisive tone, "I said about the bag. You know, if *I* were planning something, it would burn me up to not say it. Walking in silence all these miles in this godforsaken jungle, with no sign of any escape – you've noticed, I'm sure, the lack of bodies? Where are the corpses, eh? That's what *I* would do, I would speak the truth," Kane spoke quickly and not without a hint of madness in his eye.

"What truth? What are you talking about?" Bell asked baffled yet alert, scrutinizing Kane closely.

"*The* truth, what other truth could I be talking about? Whatever it is you're planning. You see, I know. I know you're hiding more. In your mind, in your bag – I know it, you *bastard!* You can't keep a secret from me, I can read your mind, I know you, I have been you. You think you know so much, but you're nothing but a stupid child!" Kane spat. The last line seemed to touch a nerve with Bell. His teeth clenched and a vein in his temple pulsed.

"What the hell are you saying? What the *hell* are you trying to say, you crazy old fool! Don't run mazes around me, just come out with it, you coward!"

"Your bag!" Kane shouted. "*What's in your bag?*"

Bell laughed, not at all from joy but purely to taunt his companion. He's trying to make me throw the first blow, Kane thought, and by God I might just!

"You paranoid fool… You belong in Bedlam, but I suppose this is the next best thing isn't it?" Bell said.

"What's in the bag, Bell?" Kane asked, but not with the heated passion that he had used only a moment before. Instead the words were slow and held a composed, icy gravity.

The two men stood in the jungle at a stalemate. A standoff. Both thought of reaching for their only weapon, yet neither did. Neither Kane nor Bell blinked, although sweat from the heat, humidity and the intensity of the moment beaded up on their foreheads. Frogs croaked irregularly and birds called and *clacked* above, yet no noise was produced by either of them.

Finally, Bell spoke sternly, calmly, evenly. "You want to know what I've been pondering, what you think I've been hiding. Here it is; why are you here, Kane? Why Honduras? You tell me money and I'll say—"

"What's in the bag, Bell?" Kane repeated.

"You're obsessed, you're a lunatic—"

"Bell, what – is – in – the – bag?" Kane said each word as a statement of its own.

"Nothing of interest to you if you can understand that!" Bell shouted. Before he could steer the conversation away, however, Kane interjected.

"Show me what else you have in your bag or I'll cut you and that bag open together, and I'll watch everything come spilling out." Kane spoke with such cold severity that Bell began to believe the man might just be serious. Bell hesitated, thinking.

"If you show me what you have in your bag too, then alright. We'll swap bags."

Kane hardly thought over the compromise before hastily agreeing, his paranoia and drive to see Bell's secrets being far too strong.

They exchanged their torn waistcoat bags, Bell keeping his hatchet by his side and Kane the bamboo fishing spear and knife. After placing the coconut water containers carefully aside, Kane quickly rifled through the coat and pulled out two items. The first was a gold-plated pocket watch. It was very aged and with a number of miniscule scratches, though overall it was well maintained. He popped it open, but nothing hid inside except an hour and minute hand, frozen in place.

The second item was bulkier and soon revealed itself as the top half of an English tea-biscuit tin. It was a painted scene of the river Thames and the numerous buildings that lined the mighty water. The bottom was rusted, but was lightly engraved 'London, love your'. The name following 'your' was rubbed and rusted beyond comprehension.

He fished around more and more, but try as he might he could find nothing else in the waistcoat. He began to shake it to see if anything would rattle or fall out. Bell looked up. He had been analyzing Kane's own belongings.

"You won't find anything else. I tried to tell you." Bell smiled, and went back to observing the two small pieces Kane had. One was a large, foreign copper coin, barely legible due to its green oxidation. Kane himself did not know what diagrams or words were within it except the year 1789 and the side portrait of a great man. A King, possibly.

The second piece was a plain gold cross, strung through a simple and thin, but broken gold chain. There were no inscriptions, and no sign of Jesus on this modest, spartan cross. Though it was by no means glistening, it had no rust and still retained an impressive level of luster. Clearly it was well cared for.

Kane watched as Bell examined the cross, a curious gleam in his eye. He slowly placed it back. With an expression impossible to read except as one deep in thought, he handed the bag back to Kane with a single "*hmph.*"

Kane, meanwhile, was distracted with the idea that while nothing sinister lay in Bell's bag, something could still be hidden in the man's pockets or on his person. Humiliation at failing to find any other weapon did little to deter Kane's conviction that Bell had an agenda concealed within him. An agenda just out of reach. It was not until Bell handed Kane back his couple of items that he was struck by Bell's countenance.

"No it… It doesn't mean anything. Doesn't make a man religious," Kane said defensively, to which Bell nodded slightly.

"Interesting," said Bell, "for a man so against God to keep such an icon as a cross."

Kane felt his chest tighten with unease.

"It's – It's nothing. It's a keepsake. It's not mine. *It's* what's important to me, not your damned God."

Bell nodded, considering Kane's explanation.

"In that case what happened to you? You were raised on God. What made you so against him?"

"Life," Kane answered, "I… I wanted to live. I

wanted adventure, to explore. And it opened my eyes. You think it's bad here? Aye, I'll agree it's bad, but it's just a taste. I've seen the world, as I always wanted to. Its splendors and its evils – and there are many evils. No God would allow such evils to happen. Not one *I* want to believe in, anyways."

Bell stayed silent. He seemed less offended then he usually would be and more contemplative of Kane's words. After a moment, Kane continued.

"You think yourself so different than me, but you have a desire for adventure and the unknown, too. You want me to believe you left your young wife behind in England and sailed across the world purely to be able to better provide? Because of better opportunities–"

"Opportunities" Bell said half-heartedly the same time as Kane, yet Kane continued.

"–Horseshit. Opportunities... you could have found those back home, or a great deal closer. You said it yourself you wanted some freedom, but it was more than that, wasn't it? Christ, doing something like you did, what if you got shipwrecked?" Kane said with a wicked smile. "How would you provide then?"

"What happened to your wife, Kane?" Bell asked, beginning to seethe.

"You don't want to know, lad," Kane said, but Bell asked again and with a renewed fury.

"What happened to your wife, Kane? Eh? What became of her?"

"I left just like you did. And when I returned…" Kane began but trailed off. He was unwilling to finish the sentence.

Bell took a step back, stunned as if someone had slapped him right then across his face. His jaw quivered with hatred.

"No," he gulped, as the terror of it all set in. "No, it can't be. I thought – I thought she had died on the Dartmouth. I thought…"

"Those were your words, not mine," said Kane, with a stab of regret at his callous willingness to let that slip. Bell turned and walked away, stumbling along their unending trail.

Kane watched the distraught man go. Bell fought against the jungle's obstacles, walking hastily, but tripped and slipped so often that he was slowed to a mere blundering crawl. Yet again, still unwilling to lose him, Kane followed Bell through the jungle. He looked up as the first few drops fell from the sky and landed on his face. A storm was approaching.

卌 卌 IIII

Kane was not wrong. The storm came and more swiftly than he could have imagined. It roared softly in the distance at first, as an angry jungle cat with no need to take another breath. Both men stopped in their tracks and with their heads bent, listened to the fury as it slowed for a moment and seemed to fall away from where it came. Within moments, however, its path suddenly reversed and the rumbling that lay deep in the jungle grew in volume and wrath and it seemed like a raging bull, heading directly for them and destroying all in its path.

"Shit – Bell!" Kane called. There was no time to use the axe to carve out a crook for a lean-to as they usually did, but there was a heavyset branch ahead of them that might function all the same. Kane motion-ed at it to Bell.

Bell, some feet ahead, turned to face Kane with eyes still laden deep with bitterness and pain. Surprise, however, quickly overcame his other emotions and he nodded and sprang to action. The drops began to fall heavier through the trees, becoming gradually more consistent. Bell and Kane ran from their location toward the beach, gathering as many fallen palm leaves as they could along the way before returning. They were not ideal, as the fronds were already drenched in water and mud from the previous rains, but they would have to do.

They had not yet returned, carrying their long, mud-draped leaves, when the fury of the storm fell on them. It came so swift and violent that although they had heard it approaching, obliterating all other sounds around them, it still rocked the men.

They were instantly beaten down by the onslaught of the storm. The volume of water was so immense that Kane felt a waterfall could not have battered them more. It fell so hard that their sight was immediately washed out and the heavyset branch they had hoped to build their shelter on became swept away in the streaky blind of the rain.

"Where are we going?" Bell shouted, barely audible above the storm.

Kane did not answer but took some steps forward. There was no time to answer, and no point. There was a massive tree just ahead, one of those that Kane often assumed housed a small town of living creatures, whether walking, crawling, flying or slith-ering. The tree had what seemed like hundreds of hardened vines draped from it, and Kane decided that it would be their best and only chance at escaping the hammering storm.

They struggled, slipping in the mud, through the storm's ferocity towards the tree. He grasped a col-lection of those vines, and tested their solidity by shoving them with whatever might he still possessed. Kane found them to be nearly as strong as their original branch. Underneath the tree the intensity of the rain lessened, but even still was powerful enough to make Kane splutter and strain to see through the endless water being thrown on his face. He dropped the palm branches and began to heave them stem first on to the vine. Bell immediately followed suit piling on his leaves as well. Within moments, a vague concept of a shelter was built – a sloppy collection of wretched palm leaves hanging in the shape of a lean-to. The men laid the last fronds on the ground under the shelter in an attempt to create something of a floor between them and the mud, and crawled in headfirst.

The first thing that they noticed was how the leaves sunk into the quagmire beneath them. The mud spilled over on the sides and rose through the gaps in the leaves. The heavens beat loudly on the low roof of their lean-to, high-pitched and with what felt like a thousand *clacks* per single moment. The waves of the wind whipped the rain diagonally and although they did their best to crouch into fetal positions in their limited space, their feet and legs, which faced the opening of the shelter, still felt the spray. Both men had water pouring off of them from their hair, their necks and their clothing. It seemed that if collected, they could have filled up a large jug with all of the water they had running off their bodies.

It was by no means cold, not the cold Kane knew could envelope Europe, but the storm had brought something of a chill. Being soaked through only made it worse. He pulled off his baggy shirt, wet and uncomfortably plastered to his chest and back. He threw it to the side and hugged his chest for warmth. Perhaps for the first time, Kane noticed how grey and brown the shirt had become. It had been white the night of the wreck.

He looked at Bell, how he sat miserably with cold clothing hugging his skin. It was far better without the wet clothing, but to hell with him, Kane thought. Whether the man was being proud, or just plain stupid, it did not matter – it wasn't his job to keep him from getting ill.

"Some shelter!" Kane exclaimed, as drops began to fall steadily from the roof on to his shoulder. He had to shout, as the incessant *clacking* drowned out his words. Kane knew that he spoke more to hear himself than to actually converse with Bell. "But we escaped the insanity! Better here than crowded under some tree, drowning in the rain. Glad we made it!"

Bell finally nodded, but his reply had Kane thinking he had neither heard nor listened to what was just said. Bell said nothing for a minute.

"How did she die, Kane?" Bell asked with a raised voice. Kane could see Bell's grief had also endured the storm.

"What?" asked Kane, pretending not to have heard. Not again, he thought. Not this. Kane looked away from Bell and around the shelter, out at the rain, trying to avoid eye contact. Kane peered up at the dripping roof. "Should really put out some containers to catch the rain off these leaves. For fresh water."

"Kane, answer my question," said Bell with dark intensity as the pounding of the rain lessened. "How did your wife die? If not the Dartmouth, then how?"

"Fever," said Kane and his throat began to seize up. "You want to know, you bastard, you won't leave me alone. She died of fever. First time I set out." Kane did not say this in anger. His words were resentful but were of a beaten manner, almost pleading.

"Fever," said Bell, nodding grimly.

"Was supposed to be a short trip," Kane continued, "a trading voyage to Gibraltar. Nothing long. Would have brought in some money and let me stretch my legs from old England a bit. She was for it, you know."

"So, she just happened to die during that short of a journey?" Bell asked skeptically.

"Well…" Kane said feebly, "there was another trade after that, a short jaunt to Malta. I wrote her, explaining. Can you pass me the containers? I'll collect some water."

"And so you returned after that trip? To Malta?" Bell asked, ignoring Kane's request for the containers.

"Aye," said Kane, heavily. "Came right home after that. It was as I arrived that I found out."

"You're lying," Bell blurted out. "You knew before."

Kane was silent. After a few moments passed he raised his head and for the first time made eye contact with Bell.

"So I did. Aye, I did. Didn't make a difference though, did it?"

"Should have stayed," Bell muttered.

"And you're so much better, are you?" Kane cried. Bell gave Kane a short, wounded look. "And if I had stayed, who's to say that I wouldn't have died of the same?"

"Well, maybe you should have!" Bell flared, and

Kane realized the man had echoed his own thoughts.

At that, Bell turned on his side with his back to Kane. The conversation ended. As Bell left Kane to ponder those unkind words, Kane felt himself begin to spiral into that all too familiar pit of guilt. Blame dealt him the uppercut. Shame hammered him down. And remorse kicked him mercilessly on the ground.

There were so many things, Kane thought. He stared up at the short, wet leaved ceiling, and yet he saw nothing. The sun had set without notice, as it does on these dark, stormy days. All he saw, staring at the ceiling, was an image of his wife from so long ago. She clung to some of the guilt buried deep inside him. But she was only the beginning, wasn't she? What would have happened had he never left? Perhaps he would have died, too. Perhaps he could have saved her. Perhaps they both would have lived and he might have stayed, miserable in that life. Yet at least she may have survived. How would his life look today had that happened? What would she say of him today, knowing all that had happened to him since? All that he had done? Kane buried his face in his hands. He did not want to know that answer.

Kane could still smell the salt and the pungent grime that hung and covered the sides of those London docks as he boarded that ship on the Thames. He had grown up seeing those masts flourish, their massive white sails carrying scores of men on those colossal floating vessels down the river and out to the world. They were everywhere that day, coming and going. He remembered feeling as if he had won a chest full of gold that day, just to have a place on one of them.

Gibraltar was not far he knew, only a fraction of the distance that he would later venture, but it felt as if it were another world – a world removed.

He remembered seeing the muck that clung to everything low-lying, and the smoke that filled the sky and marked the buildings from the riverside factories. It was as if nothing natural had ever existed there and the river had never known a life without brick and wood and smoke.

It was everything he was running from, if only for a while. Over the sea in Gibraltar he could clear his head. There he could stretch his legs and figure things out. Whatever those things had been, then. He couldn't remember now.

How he had tried to convince himself that he could remain there in England for the rest of his life. How he had purchased objects engraved with reminders of home and his life there. He had watched others remain and be happy and he was convinced he could be, too. Yet every time he saw one of those maps in the storefront, or found a foreign coin, or watched as one of those tall ships set sail for somewhere... else. He felt that tug at his heart pull harder and harder.

He had left. He had left his wife alone and he never saw her again. He had to accept it, he knew, but it had always been easier to run instead. To bury himself in some work, to accept another adventure where many would not. He believed, many times, he had little, if anything, to live for. He had no family, no son waiting back home for him. He did not have those worries that he had seen strike across other men's faces when they were perplexed with a particularly dangerous task.

He chased money and sought more and more exotic locations. Whoever offered the greatest adventure, he had told himself, was with whom he would sail. Kane grimaced at the thought.

The image of Bell staring at the golden cross bore into his mind. He knew, Kane thought, he must have. He had seen Kane's basest possession and had glimpsed into the darkest depths of his soul. Though far smaller than Christ supposedly had to carry, Kane reflected, that cross would be his to bear for the remainder of his life. Even all the way here, on the opposite side of the world and in the middle of the jungle, he could not escape it.

How could he ever escape it? How could he ever

move forward in this life? Even if he survived, somehow, what would that mean? More days to spend bearing that cursed cross.

He should have let go that night, he thought. His chest shuddered. He should have let go and joined the others in their tragedy. Perhaps it would have been a relief – for himself and for others. Why did they have to die, and some of them so brutally, yet he lived? Once again, innocents had to die and he lived on like a leech, like a parasite, clinging to life regardless of the cost.

Kane's face contorted as tears streamed hot down his cheeks. He thought again of how much he had done with the belief that he had nothing to live for. And yet he was so afraid of dying now. He did not need kin to be afraid of death. He was terrified without them. His situation was dire, hope was bleak, and he was absolutely petrified. There were no bodies. None. Unless they had missed them, which he knew was next to impossible, not a single clue that they were heading the right way existed. Which... could only mean they had made the wrong call. Days and days ago, back on that beach where he had met Bell, the wrong path had been chosen. All this way and there would be nothing but more trees and more coasts. He would find nothing but endless coast and endless trees until he finally dropped of starvation or disease and joined the soil.

He clenched his teeth in the shelter, the storm continuing its rage on their poor roof. It was too late to go back now. Far, far too late. In any sense.

Whether he physically was he could not tell, but Kane had the sensation, in the pitch dark of the rainstorm, that he was sinking deeper into the mud that lay under him, inch by inch. He could feel the mud start to envelop him, over his shoulders, his sides, his neck. The earth began to take back what was rightly hers.

And then – as if by miracle, one of the leaves holding off the storm above Kane gave out a loud *crack!* It splashed the small pool of water it had gathered down on Kane's face. He jerked upright, swearing and cursing. He felt around for the leak, yet strangely he could find nothing. No more water fell through and it was as if whatever had cracked in the leaves had patched itself up again.

As he lay back down Kane felt himself sobered. It was as if that unexpected splash of water had woken him from a long, dark dream. One filled to the brim with self-hate. He blinked, and though he was blind in the dead of the night he began to see things differently.

He was not a leech, he realized, for clinging to life. He was not a parasite for having survived that ill-fated night and he was not one for staying alive all these days since. Holding on to life and grasping it with every finger and toe he possessed was merely a characteristic of the living. And what good, what use would he be if he were dead? There was time enough, should he survive, to right some wrongs. Surely there was.

What he needed was to let go. Unbearable as it might seem, it was time for him to let go of it all. Only, not in that sense.

ЖЖ ЖЖ ЖЖ

The wind whipped Kane in the face as he stood next to the edge of the low, wooden rail. Nothing else lay in view aside from them. The gentle, rich blue of the sea stretched all the way to the horizon in every direction to meet the pale blue of the sky. All was blue on blue except for the lone ship, a black speck with three billowing masts sailing alone in the empty sea. It was not a large ship by any means, he thought, long and thin, but sailing low to the water with only a couple of decks beneath the main.

The smaller the gap between the two ships became, the more Kane could make out the white stripe that lay at the center of the ship. The new row of gun ports shone black and proud, and were evident even at this distance. They gave an ominous promise of quick cannon fire should any attack. How ironic and terrible, Kane mused, that a group such as them should know that they were only painted and fake.

And that a group such as them should know that today the Dartmouth would be sailing alone. A sitting duck.

They gained on the other ship slowly, but with a determined, steady pace. Kane had hardly slept the night before, but his apprehension at the coming scene kept him alert and ready. His stomach was a mess and every minute they inched closer a new knot tied itself in Kane's belly. He couldn't tell if it was the swaying of their ship on the water, something which hardly ever affected him, or whether it was another factor that made him so nauseous.

He glanced up every so often at their ship's flag high above. The red, white and blue of the union jack in the corner with red and white stripes running horizontally. He wondered when it would be taken down. It was a British merchant ship they sailed, an older East Indiaman, and it was the most perfect, diabolical tool Kane could think of. They gained slowly on their prey with the exact same flag.

This is what you wanted, Kane thought to himself. His eyes fixed on the sea vessel. For years now, conscious or not, you've been dreaming of this day. A chance at redemption, at retribution for all they had done to you. He felt the familiar darkness and craving for vengeance burn deep in his heart as he focused on those thoughts. He tried his best to ready himself.

Another minute passed and they continued to pull closer. They were close enough to see the dark specks of men on the main deck, some working the riggings, some standing at attention to the incoming ship. Strangely, the closer they sailed, the more Kane felt his hatred lessen and fear creep in. It was one thing to talk, another to plan, and as he felt now, the hardest of all to do. He ran through various scenarios once on board and how he would react to each. He knew, though, that before him lay a mist, a blanket of secrecy yet to be discovered. Man was afraid of nothing half so much as the unknown.

The crew shared Kane's feelings of uneasiness and excitement as hushed but electric conversations buzzed throughout the main deck. They were a varied group that the captain had put together for this raid. Some spoke Spanish, a few others French and Creole, and a number spoke English, however with a blend of American, English and Irish accents.

The captain stood near the back, his eye too was fixed keenly on the ship, only occasionally darting away. He wore a large, black captain's hat that extended far out over both of his ears. He donned a navy-blue coat and trousers, with long white stockings partially covering them. His shirt under the coat, however, was just a simple white seaman's shirt, but no eyeglass would be able to pick that up until they were already upon them. To the other ship he appeared a captain, which was integral, but to Kane he was merely a scrounger trying to pass himself off as a lord.

The captain and his unkempt, shrewdly eyed first mate standing to his right summoned a man. The man in turn hurried quickly under deck, shouting unintelligible words below.

Kane himself wore a Marine's bright cherry-red jacket, with high white trousers and a weathered-looking Baker rifle by his side. The jacket stifled Kane, and he felt himself sweating so heavily under the hot North African sun that he was surprised the jacket had not yet turned a darker shade of red. He had no hat or proper boots, but the jacket was all that would matter. A number of others donned these coats, and the rest dressed not much different than regular sailors. Each was heavily armed, however, and waiting.

It must have been only a matter of minutes, but it seemed hours to Kane as the two ships drew closer together. It was almost time, it must be almost time, he thought, and glanced anxiously up at the flag again, but it slumped and ruffled only a little in the light wind. It did not move one inch downward.

Kane could begin to make out faces on the main

deck, and one sailor even waved, as if in familiarity. They were on their way back from India, no doubt, and were likely drunk with their exploits and riches. Kane's loathing for them deepened.

They came even closer, sailing in along the broadside of the other ship. Kane could just make out a greeting call from one of the sailors on the other ship – and then the ground erupted beneath his feet as a staggered and earth-shattering *boom! boom! boom! boom!* rocked his eardrums. Kane hunched over, grabbing his ears in unexpected pain, but kept his eyes forward. He saw through the rising white smoke as men fell and chips of wood flew in every direction.

Kane glanced again at the flag, and saw that it flew just the same, unmoved. The bastards! They had unleashed a deadly round of grape shot directly at the main deck, firing completely by surprise. Kane could not hear the men next to him shouting and opening fire with their rifles, his ears rang too loudly. Their shots were still too far away and fell uselessly upon the side of the ship. Still clutching his ears as the smoke began to dissipate, a second volley of fire opened beneath him. The damage was minor this time, the men of the Dartmouth already taken cover.

Kane's hearing began to return and he felt as if his heart was audible to the whole crew, it pounded so heavily in his chest. He now could hear the shouts and the captain in the background yelling words of encouragement, but little was needed. Anticipation and a carnal euphoria shone through the men's eyes nearest him. They would have frightened him to death had they not been on his side.

They sailed nearer still, until the black side of the ship with its white stripe became invisible beneath them. The pockmarked and newly torn deck, the pools of blood and the gored bodies lay strewn throughout the ship's main deck. Severed ropes dangled in the wind and ripped sails flapped aimlessly over the battered scene – and yet all was quiet but one man.

The man was a Marine, judging by his similar bright red coat to the one Kane wore, but was missing one sleeve where grape shot had torn his arm off gruesomely at the shoulder. He screamed and cried and pulled himself with his one arm on the ground, as his legs seemed torn and bloodied too, seeping red through his white trousers. He let out one more horrible scream and three men to Kane's left opened fire. They largely missed with the distance between them, until the first bullet made contact and the man arched his back. The second then found its target, and finally a third and the man was silent.

With the man's killing came a chilling silence on the other ship. Kane's eyes scanned the deck for any sign of movement, but found none. It was as if the happy vessel had become a ghost ship in a matter of moments.

A blackened, steel grappling hook then flew from the right of Kane, cracked against the side of the other ship's rail and plummeted down to the water below. The man beside him swore and cursed at this failure. Another to the left threw his hook and found its mark, fastening the hook strongly to the rail. Then a whole flock of grappling hooks and ropes were being flung by a number of men, over and over until they each gripped the rail tightly, pulling the two ships even closer together.

About twenty Marines leapt from their cover with a shout, fired their rifles and charged forward toward the grappled hooks. Kane ducked as the shots rang out, but he could hear two men struck as they fell backward, shrieking in shock and pain.

Kane raised and aimed his rifle as his crewmates began firing back at the charging Marines. He hardly took the time to aim before he fired his weapon and the rifle jolted back hard into his shoulder with a loud *crack*. While he couldn't be sure about the bullet, smoke burst out of his rifle and enveloped him. Kane dropped, his hands shaking. He grabbed a clump of his hair and pulled hard with disbelief. I didn't even aim! He thought awfully. I just raised the gun in their direction and fired without aiming!

He reached in his bright red breast pocket and pulled out a tubular shaped cartridge. He quickly tore off the end with his teeth and with quivering hands but a clenched jaw, poured the shot and powder into the barrel. Shots fired around him and another man fell as Kane twisted and worked the paper down into the barrel, jamming it in good before plunging it down with the ramrod. He loaded the flint, readied himself and stood to fire again. He spotted a man nearest him. He felt excitement replace his anxiety and he even cracked a smile as he prepared his shot. He waited a moment longer, adjusting his sight. As he pulled the trigger and fired, however, the two ships crashed together. Kane's rifle flew out of his sweaty hands and tumbled down the crevasse between the two ships to the wood-littered waters beneath.

Kane stood for a moment, looking in stunned disbelief down the side of the ship. A shot struck into the rail in front of him, raining chips and splinters around him as he dove back down for cover. The ships crashed again and Kane saw a few men down the line began to leap over to the other ship, screaming and firing pistols as they did.

I've got no rifle left, Kane thought fleetingly. I need to do *something*! He watched carefully, amid the chaos, and when the two ships moved together again he stood and hurled himself over the two rails and fell shoulder-first on to the other deck. Though the battle still raged, Kane heaved a sigh of relief. A good part of him envisioned falling between the two ships as his rifle has just done. Kane gained his bearings and saw more of his crewmates make the jump over. The chaos would only increase on the enemy ship, he knew. And very quickly.

Smoke, blood and screams ran rampant over the deck as it became clear the Marines had failed in cutting the grappling hooks in time. Through the sporadic bouts of smoke, Kane could see this terrible knowledge was dawning on the enemy, too. One man in particular was so stricken with fear he looked nearly frozen as he hid behind a wooden crate.

The excitement and enjoyment that he had expected turned bitter in his mouth. He began to see these men as, well – just men. They were terrified – not all of them surely, but some were without a doubt. They had woken just this morning, Kane thought, and had no idea that they would be fighting for their very lives hours later. Of course, he thought, they could surrender. Why wouldn't they surrender? Perhaps they had already fought this far and had spilled enough blood that they were fearful of the consequences. If this was their fighting force, Kane wondered, they couldn't hold any hope in winning, could they?

As Kane watched, a man with a long blonde beard and a dirty brown bandana grabbed his shoulder.

"Listen, partner," he drawled, though he did not spare Kane a single glance. He kept his eyes on the enemy the entire time. "Either you can start killin' them redcoats, or you can join 'em face down in a pool of blood."

The man then shoved off of his shoulder, stood, fired, and ran forward. As much as Kane would normally take at the man's hostility, the warning was fair. He knew what kind of a crew this was. Yet, seeing that poor sailor so frightened and cower behind a crate, Kane wondered; how could he fire?

Remember the whip, a voice suddenly whispered in his mind. And, as so often happens to people yet so rarely is noticed, Kane's subconscious began to replay an entire scene of his life within mere moments during the battle.

̶H̶H̶H̶ ̶H̶H̶H̶ ̶H̶H̶H̶ I

Of course, it was not just words Kane remembered. Rather he remembered the sights, the sounds, and most of all the feelings from a particular moment of his past. A moment that was etched into Kane's very being, more so than his memory.

It was a wintry day and Kane stood on a brick road on the outskirts of London. The snow that had fallen days before had turned to dirty, grey ice. It now lay as an ugly mush on the sides of the road. The buildings surrounding him were of brick, with the exception of a few very old, decrepit ones of made of wood. They were massive to him, as buildings and the very world itself is to children of a young age. A foundry nearby filled the air with a burning oil and molten steel smell that Kane so often associated with his youth.

He was playing in the street with a ball, kicking and throwing it against the step outside the building where he lived. His father was out at work and his mother was upstairs in the cramped room his family occupied that year. His brother was gone, where he could not remember, but he wasn't there. Otherwise things may have gone very differently.

A group of four boys near his age turned down his street and the young Kane felt anxious at seeing these particular ones. He continued to play by the steps, however, in hopes they would pass. He nearly succeeded too, when the last one turned and took notice of him.

"Ay, look who it is! That bloody paddy all by himself," the faceless one called to the others.

"Where's your big brother, eh paddy? He upstairs?" a second sneered.

Kane turned to face them, but stayed silent. The boy in the back, not wanting to be left out of the fun, pushed himself forward.

"He isn't here! Were he here our lily pad would be calling to him right now." He then walked up to Kane, and with a great kick booted his ball down the street.

"Hey!" Kane shouted and ran down the street after his ball. It was his only one. As he came nearer to it, he looked over his shoulder. The four boys tailed him closely, their steps were hushed in the dirty snow. He ran past his ball and turned sharply left down the street. Kane sprinted as fast as he could, keeping his knees high as he was taught, he thought of a possible escape route and shot right down the next street. The icy snow got the best of him, however, and to his horror he slipped and fell on his back.

He scrambled in the snow to stand but before he could the front of a boot caught him in the side of the head. He screamed in pain and fell back down. He could only see shadows of bodies over him as a hailstorm of boots and fists struck him over and over again on the ground. Each was as painful as the last and with the abundance of blows at every inch of his body he could do little but cover his head and convulse in agony.

One of them said something but Kane could not make out what – his ears were throbbing and were flushed with blood. The others laughed at what that boy had said and suddenly they stopped beating him. Kane whimpered miserably on the ground, the snow around him red.

He looked up for a moment and saw no one in front of him. Kane tried to stand to run, but one of the boys called attention to this. Two of them lunged forward, grabbed him by his arms and held him face-first against the icy brick wall. He looked to his left and saw one of the boys running back downstairs where he apparently lived. In his hands he held something coiled and round. A sinister smile spread across the boy's face.

"What are you doing?" Kane cried out and the boys pushed his bruised and bloodied body harder against the wall.

"Ay, paddy!" he heard one yell behind him as he walked closer, and with a giggle said, "ever been whipped?"

Again, Kane did not take time to recount this memory from his youth during the chaos aboard that ship. Rather, he simply remembered the whip – and the flashes of the other scenes played back to him at random in his subconscious. All of these memories and emotions amassed to produce a pure, bitter hatred. Despite the compassionate and sympathetic thoughts he'd had only moments ago, the memory of the boys and the whip renewed the wicked anger that he'd gripped for so long in his heart. An anger targeted directly at the enemy, at the cowards behind their crates who fired at him and the others on board behind him.

Kane drew one of his long, flint locked pistols from his breast holster and watched carefully. The sides were nearly even now, as more of his crewmates came aboard the enemy deck. Soon the others would be outnumbered. One man popped up, blind to Kane as he watched too far to the left. The man fired, narrowly missing Kane. Kane swung right, stunned he had not seen the man. He quickly aimed and fired his pistol. He missed.

Kane dropped for cover behind a pile of rope and pulled out his other pistol. It was hardly a cover, he knew, but it was the best he had near him. In a flash he made the decision to leap up and run, rather than to wait and hope for cover fire. The other man would need to reload and he knew he would have only seconds to act. Kane sprinted to the side of the wooden crate where the other man hid. He found his rival with his ramrod, about to load another shot down his rifle's muzzle. The man had a dirty white top with grey trousers and as his enemy's long, blonde hair swung out of his face Kane could see the fear deep in his pale blue eyes. He would never forget those eyes nor the man's look – half pleading and half in disgust of him. The eyes, the windows to the man's soul. The blonde man's hand shot for his pocket, reaching for a weapon. He was too late, however, as Kane had already lowered his third and final pistol. Kane fired pointblank into the center of the man's chest.

The sailor fell to the ground, gasping and holding his chest as a small hatchet crashed out of his pocket beside him. Kane stood in shock for a moment, watching the blood begin to flow in spurts and spread red throughout the white shirt. The man reached for the hatchet and Kane leapt. He stomped on the man's outstretched hand with the heel of his boot and grabbed the small wooden axe with its chipped and rusty blade. With eyes wide with hatred and his mouth bellowing what could only be described as a war-cry, Kane brought the axe down with all his might on the center of the man's bloody back. He did not stop. Instead, he mechanically ripped the blade out, exactly as he used to do when an axe was stuck splitting timber, and heaved it down again and again. Each time he ripped out the blade from the man's back, recollections of his childhood would flash before him, the humiliation and the terror and the loathing, and he would howl and bring the hatchet down again, his eyes glistening with tears.

Finally, Kane stopped. The dead man's hot blood was spattered from Kane's boots to his face. A Marine stood a few paces away, his bright red coat so like Kane's, and raised his rifle. The Marine looked at Kane as if he were staring at the Devil himself. As if Satan had personified here on Earth and he was ready to banish the demon back to hell. Before he could, however, a sudden blast of smoke came from the Marine's left and the soldier fell. The pirate who had dealt the blow ran up, pistol in hand and finished the man off.

Kane looked back down at his victim, his back a bloodied and savaged pulp. No trace of his shirt suggested it had ever been white. He thought of what the American had said, about being dead and face down in a pool of blood. That was exactly how this man now lay before him. He was about to turn away when the hot, bright sun above reflected a shimmer off the dead man. Kane bent down to take a closer look and saw that one of his hatchet blows had severed a gold chain that had hung round the man's neck. He did not know why he did it, whether it was for a souvenir of the battle, a remembrance of that moment of his life when he had exacted his revenge, or something to remember the poor man by, but he pulled the chain with its dangling pendant and stuffed it deep into his pocket. It was not until later that he would see the simple cross that adorned the chain.

Something was different, Kane realized, as he tore himself away from his victim. With his entire body shaking from the sobering of his own brutality, he realized that the firing had stopped. The fighting, as quickly as it began, seemed to be over. Only one sailor still stood, revealing himself up on the higher forecastle deck. He raised his rifle high above his head.

"I surrender! Please! I surrender!" the man shouted.

"It's alright, come on down lad, we won't hurt yeh," an Englishman shouted back, slowly rising from his cover. "Just put the rifle down!"

The sailor did exactly as ordered and with his hands up walked slowly toward the English pirate. His trousers began to stain and drip as he walked. The pirate strolled up to the man.

"Turn around, and I'll tie yeh," the pirate ordered, and the sailor did, holding his hands out to be tied. Instead of rope, however, the pirate drew his pistol and fired a shot to the back of the man's head. The body dropped instantly to its knees and then to the deck, unaware of its demise. Kane normally would have been shaken by the brutality, but being already in such a frenzied and surreal state of shock, he merely watched the event take place as if they were actors in a play.

With a loud pop, Kane noticed a small fire begin to crackle and burn near the stern of the ship. How had it started? He had not seen nor noticed anything, but then he wouldn't have, being absorbed in his corner of the battle. Yet there it was, licking orange and red into the air and wafting a thick black smoke through the aftermath of the battle.

Kane saw the captain and the first mate, now aboard and involved in discussion. Men all around him began to talk, in English, French and Spanish. He could hear two Americans nearby speaking loudly with manic, post-bloodshed excitement in their eyes.

"So, what do you think we'll find below, huh? Gin or tea, I bet."

"Are you blind? Do you not see the fire? This ship's carrying saltpeter, or some goddamn material. Whole fucking vessel is probably a floating tinder box."

The two men then strode away and toward the trap door that led below to the berth deck. As their conversation pulled out of Kane's hearing, something else came into it. It was only dim at first, yet very familiar. It soon grew quite loud until it was smothered. It was a child's whimpering cry through the boards beneath him.

It was enough to rip Kane out of his stunned stupor. *Jesus Christ!* A panic gripped him and he felt his heart drop through his stomach down to his feet. Were there children on board? He swung out his hand and grabbed the crewmate nearest him, a man with a brown shirt and a salt and pepper beard.

"Did you hear that? Are there children on this ship?" Then another thought occurred to him. "Children and women? Eh? Are there?"

But the man looked incomprehensibly at Kane

and shrugged off his grasp, walking off with a swagger. The man doesn't speak English, Kane realized, as the pirate bent down and flipped over a body, searching it for jewelry and other valuables.

"Captain!" Kane shouted to their commander, who kept his hat on with something of a smug vanity. The captain was the one with the plans and the prior information. It was he who knew the gun ports were merely painted on to frighten away pirates, and he who knew the Dartmouth would be alone today. "Captain – are there any children aboard? Captain!" But the captain just gave Kane an irritated sideways glance before turning away to face the crew near the trapdoor. The trapdoor that lead to the berth deck below.

"What are yeh waiting for?" he shouted. "Get yerselves down there and find the cargo! And what and who ever else yeh find… Is yers fer the keeping." He smiled his sickly, rotten smile at this last line.

God! Kane thought, *he knows!*

Next, however, something went terribly wrong. It was a simple mistake, which regardless of the many hours the Captain had spent pouring over the battle plans would have been difficult, if not impossible, to account for. It was one rogue dynamic among so many possible factors that come with having such wild men as your crew – and in one unexpected moment everything was ruined.

The man nearest the trapdoor that led to the berth deck below ripped open the door with great bravado. As the door opened a soul-crushing chorus of screams flooded the air. It was as if the door was keeping them contained all this time, and only now the shrieks, cries and shouts were free to fill the skies above.

The man who opened the door wore a red bandana covering his hair and had bloodstains on his dirty white shirt. He had his sleeves rolled to his elbows showing a number of skeleton tattoos. Though far away, his trimmed, black moustache widened with his smile as he turned to the crew. His was another image Kane would never be able to shake.

"By the authority of the King," he said, mocking the British East India Company's slogan, and from behind his back revealed a weapon, "and the parliament of England."

The man with the bandana held in his hand a black ball, with a hissing wick spouting out of it – and Kane realized to his horror it was a live explosive.

"What are you d – no, no, no, no, NO!" Kane cried as he ran towards the man, but his effort was too little and too late. The man flung the explosive down to the deck below.

The apocalypse then fell on the HMS Dartmouth.

The deck surrounding that door erupted upwards in an explosion of smoke, fire and shredded wood. A board slammed sideways into Kane's chest, knocking him down and leaving him gasping for air. He sat up on one elbow and watched the destruction unfold in front of him. Pieces of the ship rained down around him as smoke and fire towered up out of the newly created crater that dug deep through the ship. Flames licked and spread through the sails, turning the Dartmouth into a massive, floating pyre. The ship of the damned, Kane thought, watching the charred and bloodied bodies around him in amongst the flames and raining carnage from the explosion.

Haunting, awful screams and desperate pleas rose out from the newly formed fiery crater. The ship began to sink and Kane wondered if there was not something he could still do for those below. Some of them could still be saved! Yet, as the ship drew lower and the flames flew higher out of that hell-like pit, he felt himself utterly helpless to the suffocating weakness holding him back. Kane submitted, like a slave, to the power his weakness held over him. He dragged himself up off the deck, and with those of the crew that survived, he pulled himself to the edge of the ship. The ropes that grappled the ships together began to grow longer and steeper as the Dartmouth sank downward.

"And now I've seen hell." The words rather slipped from his mouth than were actually spoken, as Kane glanced back one last time at the devastation.

HHt HHt HHt II

Kane awoke to a set of ear-piercing squawks drowning out the regular rhythm of the jungle. Two bright green Lora birds flew far above the tree canopy, alerting the surrounding jungle and its inhabitants as to their passing. He covered his eyes with a hand and rubbed at them groggily. As he opened them all was bleary. Gradually, he could make out thin beams of bright sunlight shining through the leaf-thatched roof of the shelter. It was as if the light was spread finely with a knife. Drops still spattered at random from the previous night's storm and pools of water that had built up in leaves could be heard emptying sporadically.

Strange, thought Kane. Typically, he awoke to the sounds of the howling monkeys at dawn, when the day's light was still only dim. To hear those birds meant that it was much later.

As Kane's vision to his surroundings became clearer, the memory of his dream the night before grew steadily vaguer, as dreams always do, until he was left with nothing but the raw emotion that had gripped him in the dream world and stayed with him in this one. The hollowness of hunger he felt in his stomach was made only worse by the deep, heavy hole that lay in his chest from his dream. He did not have to remember the dream to know what it was about. He heard those screams and felt that eruption under his feet every single day.

Kane blinked as he watched two ants make their way upside down at the top of the thatched roof. Ever since that fateful day off the North African coast he was a man haunted. The feeling of guilt, the pure and absolute shame, returned like a spear to his belly, slashing and tearing at his insides. And there was nothing he could do.

Yet as another drop fell, he remembered the resolution he had made the night before. He felt a light shine through the darkness of his soul, remembering this. The darkness, however, was the resident. The light only a visitor. He could already sense the resolution fading. It was impossible, was it not?

Immediately Kane grew aware of something else — an familiar force causing an uneasiness in him that lingered just beneath the surface of his detection, but now became painfully clear. He jerked his head upright and looked out the entrance of the small shelter. Sure enough it was there that Bell sat, his arms wrapped around his knees, staring at Kane.

At first glance, Kane saw a steely cold hostility in Bell's face as the man looked on at him. There was bitter contempt in Bell's lowered eyelids, clenched jaw and furrowed brow – but all that changed in an instant as Bell noticed Kane watching him. His entire expression altered in a flash, becoming a relaxed and good-natured countenance. Bell's jaw loosened, his eyes widened and his brow lifted as he spoke to Kane.

"Morning, sailor! What's for breakfast?"

Kane pulled himself up and rested on his elbows. The cheery, friendliness of this greeting startled Kane a little. The words were pleasant enough, but the tone behind them had a forced quality that sent a shiver down his back. He would have almost preferred if Bell had spoken to him with that hostility he had seen on his face only a moment ago. The words would have been more sincere. Regardless, he thought, the game had been chosen and he would play along.

"Considering what we have for food, I guess I'll have sunshine," Kane said, gruffly. The world beyond the triangular entrance to their shelter was an illuminated, vibrant green. "Given all the rain and sunshine we've had, figured you would have grown a foot or two more by now, Bell."

"Because I'm like a bean, is that it old man?" Bell looked amused.

Kane shrugged and pulled himself out of the thatched shelter, taking in the world around him. Drops fell so plentifully everywhere from the leaves to the muddy ground, that he thought for a moment it was in fact still raining. The blue sky above, however, was strong enough to make its way, in pieces, though the many leaves and trees that did their best to hide it.

As he stood, Kane winced and looked down at the cloth that bandaged his wounded feet. They were tied well, as only a sailor could.

"Your words, not mine," Kane replied.

Normally, that would have been it for conversation. They would have looked at what pieces of coconut they could scrape out from what little that was left, have some water, see if there were any fruit bearing trees nearby, and begin another painfully slow hike. But nothing about today was normal.

"So... Kane?" Bell said, still amicable enough, but giving Kane the feeling the man was coming to some point that had been decided on from before he awoke.

Kane waited, but Bell did not continue. Instead he stood with a complexity on his face, the words on the tip of his tongue.

"Well, what?" Kane blurted out, "Back to the

questions, is it?"

Bell's face ruffled a bit at Kane's coarseness of response.

"What in your dream was hell?" Bell asked, more straightforwardly.

"My – my what? My dream?" Kane was taken aback. "Why are you asking me about my dreams? What's… what's got into you? Do I ask you about your dreams?"

Bell did not answer at first. Instead, as he did more and more these days, he watched Kane with that same inquisitive, untrusting face.

"I don't dream. You must know that," he said flatly. "I'm only asking because you repeated the word 'hell' over and over again, gasping at your own words."

"Hell? I said 'hell'?" Kane asked, with a faltering strength. "I must have… I must have been dreaming about our situation. Wouldn't you say this is a hell of a situation?"

Again, Bell paused before responding.

"I would. I would say this is a hell of a situation. We haven't seen any more bodies, any pieces of the wreck – nothing, not for days. It's more than a hell, our situation, it's a damned catastrophe. Only… I said so from the beginning. But it was not long ago that you were the damned jungle God's disciple, wasn't it?" Bell thought for a moment and squinted his eyes before continuing. "In fact… you've got this look on your face, like you've done something. Something horrible – probably why you're here in the first damn place. I've noticed it for some time, but I've left it alone. I thought it was your wife, your…" Bell's voice faltered for a moment on this, but quickly regained strength. "I thought that was it. That's something a regular man might regret. But you're no regular man, are you, Kane? No, you've done something worse, much worse – and for a while now I could only guess. But then," Bell stared directly into Kane's eyes, as much as Kane tried to avert his own, "but then you lied about the cross." said Bell, bitterly.

Kane nearly leapt at the mentioning of the cross.

"I didn't – I didn't lie about any damned cross! That's a keepsake! I told you it's not mine!"

"Who's it from, then? Your keepsake?"

"Doesn't matter, does it? It's… my grandfather's. One of the few things he gave me," Kane replied, and though he spoke without the slightest wavering, his face showed intense concern on the subject. A concern he could not hide.

"Your grandfather's cross," Bell nodded. "You had a protestant grandfather, then?"

Kane blinked.

"A what?"

"A protestant grandfather. Hadn't you noticed? The cross is as plain as porridge. There is not the slightest hint of Catholic in it, no sign of Jesus, not even a bloody indent. And you want me to believe that your Catholic, chest-thumping, Irish grandfather passed on a protestant cross with a shattered chain to his grandson? Make any sense to you, paddy?"

Kane's blood drained from his face and he felt a wildfire of panic spread throughout his body.

"It's… No, I can explain, you see… It's"–

"I'm not finished," Bell said, and with each word he seemed to gain a greater and greater disdain for the man in front of him. "See, I'd watched this face you've had, this regret about something. Not your wife. No, though I'm sure some regret lies there, as it should. But this was something else that I saw, though I could not yet understand what. When I held that cross yesterday, though, I saw that face, that regret, so intensified I could hardly believe it. It made no sense, it was just a stolen piece of jewelry. Perhaps to me it's of religious significance, but to you that's all it would be. And then I remembered. You claimed you had actually been on the Dartmouth. *On the bloody Dartmouth of all ships!* I thought it was maybe a fantastical claim, meant to impress me, or maybe you really had survived. I'd read those papers, though, piece after piece, and found it difficult to believe any of the victims could have survived. They say it was stocked with all the components of gunpowder, making it a ship-sized explosive. It all became clear then. You came here, to Honduras, the wildest part of anything British in an attempt to hide your shame. But I know you. I know who you are. You are the worst scum to walk the Earth. You're a *pirate!*"

Kane felt as if each sentence Bell spat pushed him closer and closer to the edge of an invisible cliff. His last words gave him the final shove over that figurative edge.

"No! No, no, no, no, no... I'm not – I was never one of them, I just – I signed on for one – just one! – but..."

"Does it matter, Kane? One or twenty or a hundred, does it really matter now?" Bell asked, quieter now, his voice thick with desolation. "You kill and you become a murderer. You might live on now, like the roach that you are, but never again will you not be a child murderer. You will always have killed those poor people. There is no escaping that. Doesn't matter if you are standing on London Bridge, or in the center of the jungle. It will always be true."

Kane was hunched over now, his chin on his knees and his fingers running feverishly through his long, matted hair. Tears began to streak down his face.

"Stop it, stop it, Bell. Just stop. You don't know what you're talking about…"

"Oh I don't know what I'm talking about? Is that what you said, you disgusting worm? Oh, I know exactly what I'm talking about, unless you've forgotten. How… How I wish I did not. But now I know exactly what my future brings. Every miserable detail… Tell me though, Kane, why did you do it? Was the hate so hard to deal with? You realize they weren't the ones that hurt you, they weren't the ones that killed your brother."

"I know," Kane sniffed, tugging on his hair, "I know they weren't. But that hate, that constant torment inside… It never went away! But, but, I can learn – I can learn from my mistakes!"

"And you think you deserve to learn, do you? Do those on the Dartmouth get a second chance? Eh? You should have died with those who were eaten by the sharks."

"I know," Kane nodded miserably.

"And you know what I would have done had I come across your body? I would have smiled for two reasons: First because I would know I was heading the right way towards the wreck. And second, because the world would be free of one more loathsome, evil man."

Kane's felt each wretched blow at these words

break him down to such a low, dark place, that the light shining down through the trees above him seemed miles and miles away. He was trapped, down in a dark, dank well, and sinking further into the mud. This desperation and helplessness sparked a sudden fire in him, and he leapt up from his crouched, desperate position to look Bell in the eyes with a blazing fury.

"Shut up! SHUT UP!" he roared, and clenched his fists. Bell did not back down, however, and stepped even closer, coming toe to toe with Kane.

"Want me to shut up, eh paddy? Want to shut me up, like you shut up all those before you? No, I won't go away. You can hide from your family, from your country and all you know, but I will always be with you. I am not going anywhere. Understand this, Kane. As much as you would like to still believe it, you are not the good guy. You can't be a part of something like that and still claim to be a moral being. You are a thief, you are a bandit, and you are a murderer. You are the sick, twisted villain of the story of our lives. You could have been anything – anything, you realize! You could have been how you always dreamed… But instead you became this worthless creature! *I* could have been anything, but now my part is written. And I have no choice…"

"No," Kane shook his head and felt a rush of

emotions flowing through him. Anger, sadness, hope, all washed through his veins as he made his decision. His voice began to break as he spoke. "I'll always be the villain to you, Bell. And I am sorry. I can never apologize enough for what I've done and I know your life will not be what and how you dreamed it. But I can still change. And that… That's the best I can do. The best I can do for those poor ones, the best I can do for myself, and the best I can do for you. But I know, I know I will always be the villain to you." Kane looked down then, at the items scattered around the ground. First, he saw the gold cross pendant on the severed chain, then the old tin of the River Thames and the pocket watch his wife had given him those years ago, the old foreign coin he was gifted as a child and, lastly, the rusty hatchet. "That's why it's time I let you go."

Bell did not have time to say another word before Kane lunged forward and tightly gripped the hatchet.

卌 卌 卌 III

Kane pushed a large fern leaf aside and ducked under a low branch that twisted and turned like a snake through the midair. The jungle was as alive as ever, with its multifarious shouts, calls and sounds – and yet it was oddly silent. Kane stopped a moment, scanned the terrain ahead, decided the best path and continued his unending hike.

Minutes into his trek, however, Kane came to a tree and stopped. There was nothing remarkable about this particular tree. Dozens of similar trees grew throughout the jungle around him, yet this one gripped Kane. He studied it as one might a famous painting in an art gallery. It loomed over Kane as he studied the leaves that flourished through the branches. Some were just sprouts, tiny buds that had hardly left the branch and had only just entered the world. Some were great, vivacious and green, while others were fading shades of yellow, red and brown.

Kane looked at his feet. Then there were the dead leaves that littered the forest floor. He stood a moment longer in contemplation of this before continuing on.

Everything was the same and yet all had changed. It was difficult for Kane to comprehend what had altered, but it was as if the air seemed fresher, the sounds more distinct and crisp. Even the colors were brighter. Though he could not fully grasp what he was feeling in that moment, he would later come to understand it as freedom. It was the first moment in so many days and nights, sailings and landings, months, but more likely years, that he felt his mind at such peace. There was no accusing, no doubting, no agonizing despair or feelings of worthlessness.

He thought back to that moment on the beach, mere days after the wreck, when he had summoned up memories of his past life, the man he used to be. He sought comfort in this, but found such pain instead. He thought of all the times that had pained him; leaving his wife, the battle on the Dartmouth, times that would have made him cringe with shame before. Now, however, he understood them for what they were. Those moments defined him once, perhaps, but no longer. He did not forget them, but he did not keep them and their ruinous judgment side by side with him anymore.

The image of the man with the lively green eyes and long, shaggy brown hair flashed before him and Kane felt a small pang of loneliness as he looked around him and saw not a soul. What was it he missed? Surely it was not Bell, but in a way he had grown so accustomed to having that sorrowful side of him around that he felt quite alone now. It was as if a piece of him, a piece that made him *him*, negative and hurtful as it was, was abruptly gone and nothing was there to take its place. That piece of him, like an organ, had been removed and all that was left was an empty gap in his body.

A strong bout of depression fell swiftly on Kane. Perhaps this freedom, this liberation, was not worth it after all? What good was it, if he was not happy? He shook his head at the irony. I hated Bell, he thought, and I know he hated me. He hated me intensely, and yet… and yet a part of me misses him. He began to wonder that if he could go back, would he not have done it?

With that thought, however, Kane was sharply taken aback. He could have slapped himself in the face. You are free! He thought, and shouted to the jungle and ocean around him.

"I am free!"

But then… why did he feel this way? He had torn out his demon and yet he felt such a conflict of joy and sadness that he was nearly dizzy.

A warm, humid wind blew through the jungle, and the drooping leaves, branches and hanging vines above him parted momentarily, brightening the ground ahead of Kane. It was not Bell, he realized. Yes, a part of him missed Bell, as one misses anything that was once familiar. Yet Bell was not what steeped him in such disillusionment. It was that even without Bell, even without his chains of oppression that dragged him down for so long, *he was still heading for the wreck.*

His feet hurt so badly, both externally from the network of slits and cuts he had sustained, and internally from the relentless walking day after day, that his every step was a throbbing obstacle to overcome. His stomach growled as if an angry jungle cat walked with him, endlessly snarling. If only he could stop and spend another day fishing with his spear, he thought. He did not know how he would make a fire in this damp jungle yet, but he could eat his fish raw in in the meantime and soon enough he could learn.

There were no more bodies, Kane thought, but not bitterly as before. Instead he contemplated this with a calm understanding. There were no visible signs he had seen to even *suggest* he was heading the right way towards the wreck! So, why beat his body down into a daily pulp just to find another beach, or scale another hill with no point or purpose?

As Kane thought on the subject of the wreck, his thoughts grew stronger and with passion; *I don't want to find the wreck!* Even if he found it, he realized, he would not wait for help. To hell with the help! What help did being part of that world ever bring him? What good? What happiness? Sure, he might gain a meal, and a hammock, but within days he would arrive at another English land, another settlement, another god damn society! A society built on lumber, no less. One whose sole purpose was to rip out the jungle, *this* jungle, *my* jungle, and strip it of its lifeblood. All to send some wood back to the empire. They would rip out the beating heart of this land and send it away to be bastardized as they bastardized everything! And those people, Kane internally fumed, those people that populated the place he had chosen to hide, were nothing but thousands of Bell's, weren't they? They were there to make a little money while the empire made heaps, and like Bell they would look on these sacred lands with blind eyes... They would not see what *he* saw.

I don't need them, thought Kane – not their money, not their society, not their corrupt rubbish civilization – none of it! He fished through his waist-coat-satchel and began to pull out its few remaining belongings. He ran his thumb lightly over the hatchet. He felt the splintered wooden handle and the blade with its flecks of rust as they ran over the ridges of his thumb. I have this, he thought. I have a hatchet, a spear and a knife. I could build a small shelter here, somewhere, maybe next to the nearest river. There would be plenty of bamboo, palm leaves for thatching, coconuts fiber for bedding. Kane gingerly stepped over a small fern, and then another. *It could work,* he thought with a small but building excitement deep in his chest. It really could!

He began to imagine what that house and his life in it would look like. The more he imagined this, the more his excitement began to build and blossom into an intense happiness and a feeling that he had not encountered in so long it felt strange to experience once again. A feeling of peace. With this lightness and elation in his heart he began to find the simplest yet best answers to every question his mind could muster. With fish from the river, fruit from the trees, and roots from underground he would not go hungry. He would have plenty. At first he would have to find the trees and the roots and the best places to fish, but given time he would. He could cultivate the trees around his future house, he could have a garden, there, in the middle of it all.

He would make fire, and *god* how nice it would be! If the natives of the land did come, as he feared so much before, finding him from the smoke of his fire, he would not worry. He would befriend them, or do his best to. He could give them gifts so they would understand he was not one of *them*. He could show them another side to the white man, a side not driven by money, or greed, or fear, or hate. But rather one that loves their land as much as they do.

Even if he were to die in this jungle, whether by snake, wildcat, poisonous insect, sickness, or human hand – even this did not frighten him anymore. This was what separated him from Bell, and the Bells of the world. He was a part of this life all around him, not separate from it. He understood this, perhaps subconsciously perhaps before, but now he knew deep within himself, as such insightful understandings can only be *felt*, not known. He was one with the nature. He was not above it, nor detached from it or in control of it, but merely a puzzle piece in a much larger picture. Along with the monkeys, the snakes, the birds, the frogs, the insects, and all the vegetation, he was a part of this myriad of life. Alien as he appeared to this world around him, he was neither better nor worse than any of the other inhabitants, and he took a surprising comfort in that.

He glanced down at his feet again, the mud covering the bandages around them. Through the throbbing pain Kane smiled. I no longer need to trek, he thought happily. I still will of course, but rather out of choice than necessity. He would go on to find his new home, to find the base for his new life. Not a salvation in the form of a wreck, the lifeless hull of a drown ship. He would leave that life, and all of its comforts and pains behind in that far away land.

Kane stopped a moment and took in his surroundings. Another small coastline lay just ahead. It was covered by large ferns and low hanging trees and vines, but the rolling sound of crashing waves suggested it lay not too far away. Kane grinned to himself as he felt the warmth of the sun fall through an opening above him and melt the cold, bitter hardness that he kept inside. He listened to the chorus of *chirps, ribbits* and *squawks,* and welcomed them as the sounds of his new home. It was so unlike the carriage jostling, horse clopping and people shouting that he was used to!

He walked confidently toward the beach, brushing aside ferns and vines. As always, he stayed wary of snakes and spiders as he stepped around the foliage. Perhaps there would be a river here. Maybe this would be where he would settle? Who knew? His thoughts were bustling with excitement.

Kane brushed aside the last vine and stepped through to the beach — and there he saw it. His eyes scrambled to take in all of the sights at once and his body froze as if instantly turned to stone. In front of him lay a small, narrow cove with a pebbly beach upon which white water swirled and disappeared into the rocks.

Along the edges of the beach, piled in four heaps, lay a grisly, macabre scene of lifeless, bloated bodies. They were so distorted by their fate and exposure to the elements that it was difficult to believe life had ever breathed into them, let alone weeks before. A body lay on top of the pile nearest Kane, its skin a pale blue-green and its head lolled backwards to face him. The corpse had no eyes, just empty sockets, and its mouth hung wide open, as if in a permanent state of shock as to its fate.

In the center of the pebbly beach was a single rowboat, manned by three men in bright red jackets and cream-white pants that Kane felt he knew from a past life to be Marines. The fourth was a ragged, depraved looking man with his back bare and his clothes discolored and tattered. The men were all deep in conversation.

And there, far out in the background of this senseless scene lay the remains of a wooden ship. It stood like a scar upon the landscape, lay split and carved into two adjacent pieces that staggered upwards upon a group of treacherous, shallow rocks. The wreck of the HMS Vigil glistened in the sun as the waves broke upon the wood and stone.

A gust blew strongly behind Kane and out to the sea, pushing him to take one step forward. And for the first time since Kane appeared on the beach, the men at the rowboat took notice of him.

HHI HHI HHI IIII

The waves of the bay rolled heavy onto the gritty shore. The surf hissed, almost unwillingly, as the water was dragged back into the ocean only to be thrown again, hammering the beach pebbles relentlessly. Insects chirped and rang through the jungle behind Kane as he stood on the precipice between the two worlds. The sky was clear blue and the fiery sun burned into his skin.

The wind shifted, from blowing out to sea toward inland instead, and the smell of the rotting bodies turned with it. Later, Kane would remember that in all his life he had never smelt anything so nauseatingly putrid. And yet, Kane was deaf and dumb to all of it. He stood like a man who had been hit over the back of the head with a club. His jaw lay slacked and his mind flailed, trying to grasp the reality of the situation.

He turned and moved to slip back under those

vines and into the jungle. Every part of him felt repelled from the scene, as if by invisible force. He could slip back unseen, he thought frantically. His home was not yet lost, he could still find it, still build that small piece of Eden just for himself, and he could still be one, one with the nature and the –

"Oi!" he heard from behind him and again Kane froze. "Turn around!"

Kane's stomach dropped inside of him. He stared at the vines ahead, there just steps away, and through the branches and the greenery he could see that patch beyond, where the leaves parted and the sun beamed down upon that divine piece of jungle. There where he had just stood!

"Turn around now or we will fire!" the voice behind him boomed again.

Kane's muscles tensed and his jaw clenched and unclenched. It was not lost yet, he said to himself, it was not lost yet –

But enough time had passed and for fear of the voice Kane turned slowly around. There, far away but close enough, stood the three Marines, their rifles raised and aimed directly at him. He dropped his bamboo spear.

"Are you English?" the Marine in the center shouted.

Kane stared at them in disbelief, and while he did

not run back into the jungle, he made no other movement either. Though the cover of the jungle was mere steps behind him, he began to feel that his river, his home and even the very vines he had only just stepped through were already miles away.

"English or not? I swear to God if you do not answer me we will fire!" the Marine bellowed over the distance between them.

Kane hesitated, but as the *click* of that Marine's rifle sounded, he replied, "I'm English!" in a raspy, throaty voice. A voice unused for many days.

The Marine watched Kane a moment.

"Are you alone?" he asked.

Kane began to shake his head, but corrected himself.

"Aye, alone."

"Step closer!" And Kane began to slowly make his way toward the men by the rowboat.

As he came closer, however, the ragged man with sweat soaked hair pointed his finger at Kane and shouted in fear. His face and bare chest were deep brown, both from the sun and from flecks of dirt and sand that covered his body and his tattered pants. A tattoo ran across his chest and was only just visible under the dirt. He scrambled backwards, behind the Marines.

"It's him! It's him!" he cried.

The Marines glanced back and forth between Kane and the man, clearly uneasy over the sudden panic of the man they had just rescued.

"Who?" demanded the head Marine. "Who is he?"

"I know him! I know who he is!" The ragged man exclaimed, cowering behind the three men.

Kane then realized that he, too, knew who this man was.

"*How*, do you know him, you fool? Who is he?" the head Marine snapped, growing visibly annoyed.

"He chased me, sir. He chased me like a madman through the jungle only yesterday. He wanted to *kill* me! He's not one of us! He's a *devil!* A *savage!*" Although there was still considerable distance still between them, Kane could see the whites of his eyes as he said these last words.

The head Marine looked unsure as to how to proceed, and shifted his gaze from Kane to the ragged man as if they were both insane.

"Were you on the ship before it wrecked?" he finally asked Kane, who was walking steadily closer.

"Aye, I was on that bastard…" Kane muttered. He gazed out at it, shredded and torn on the ocean, split in two as if it now formed the gates to hell. He then thought of the bodies piled around him. It wasn't such a bad reference.

"Louder!" the Marine yelled.

"Aye!" Kane replied with irritation. Soon he came close enough that shouting became unnecessary and said, "aye! Me English savage on ship! Look gentlemen, if you're going to kill me after surviving all those days in the jungle then just fire. Let's see some smoke and fire those bastards! Otherwise put those god damn things away."

The head Marine glanced at the other two, nodded, and the men stood at ease. Now that he was nearer Kane could see the head Marine was a bull of a man. He had a wide, thick forehead with a vein throbbing across it, a large, thick neck, and a uniform that only just constrained his bulky figure within it. He did not look pleased at his rescue mission. He seemed like a man with orders he did not much care for but was forced to abide by.

"Did you run at this man, here, and shout at him?" the Marine asked gruffly. Kane glanced at the cowering figure behind the Marine.

"Aye."

The Marine sighed.

"And why?"

Kane shrugged. A hundred things he wanted to say, but instead he glanced at the rifles and spoke quietly.

"You spend some time in there, and you'll see

why."

Kane had finished walking the length of the beach and stopped in front of the head Marine. He stared directly into the soldier's eyes, a boldness the man was clearly displeased with. The bull of a man stared insolently back, his eyes flicking from spot to spot on Kane's face, scrutinizing him.

"You could be more grateful, like your mate here," the Marine sneered as he motioned to the recoiled, shabby man behind him. "He was practically hopping up and down on shore for us to come in."

Kane took a look at the man. He looked like a terrified animal, his eyes wide with fear. He looked ready to bolt and scurry away at the slightest notice.

"He is not my mate," Kane said, looking back into the Marine's eyes, and then said flatly and without feeling, "and I *am* grateful."

The Marine stared a moment more with an impertinent air into Kane's eyes before turning away.

"You'll help us push this boat back out to sea then," he said, and motioned to the other Marines and they turned to take their positions behind the rowboat. As they turned, the head Marine spoke to the other two.

"Only two after all this time... No point in waiting for any others. We'll report to the captain once aboard that we're free to leave."

Kane thought one of the Marines, a young man with short, dark hair and a soft face, might have objected, so concerned and torn was his face. Instead he only nodded and lowered his head.

"Ah, one last thing before we leave," the head Marine turned to Kane, "I will need your name for the log onboard."

"Kane," he answered.

The Marine sighed, "full name, man, if you please."

"Kane Seamus Bell," Kane replied.

The Marine's eyes pinched into a squint at the sound of his name. For a moment Kane's stomach tightened at the reaction. An image of the Dartmouth flashed before him.

"Seamus Bell? A paddy name? Not really English, then, are you?" he scoffed and cracked a mocking smile. The other two Marines chuckled. On some level Kane felt the intended insult, but was in too much of a daze to react or care. Besides, his was not a position to be reacting.

Instead Kane felt as if things were moving much too quickly. He was still struggling to grasp the scene he found himself in, and though he walked slowly, as if to try and slow things down further, time sped onward. He pushed the back of the rowboat, alongside the others, into the waves that broke on the shore. The waves were strong, but the boat was heavy, and with the strength of the men behind it they managed to bring it deep enough until the warm water pushed back and forth on their stomachs. First the Marines pulled themselves over and into the boat. One then grabbed the ragged man, plucking the light body under those tattered clothes and flung him on board. Lastly, as Kane tried to steal a glance backward at the shore, one of the other Marines grabbed him under the armpits and threw him head first into the boat.

Two Marines, not the head Marine but the subordinates, manned the oars. The boat rocked sharply up before plummeting down wave after wave as they pulled out of the surf and into calmer waters.

Kane sat near the back of the rowboat, in the middle, and watched the greenery beyond that stony shore in silence. The skies were a deep blue, with little wisps of white clouds strewn here and there. Clumps of palms towered, their green, yellow and orange leaves swayed and ruffled with the breeze. Tall, deeply rooted trees swathed in thick oval leaves flanked both sides of the bay and stretched out over the water. From this angle Kane felt as if they were calling to him, reaching out a hand to a fallen friend.

Kane glanced over at the ragged man. The man watched nothing, not the ever-expanding shoreline, or the wrecked ship, or the rustling waters – nothing but him. As Kane took notice of this the wary eyes of the man increased in their distrust, as if still expecting that at any moment the demon that had chased him through the bush would reappear.

"What, you think I'm still going to chase you?" Kane asked, almost amused by the man's fear. "Where? Where would you go if I did? Are you going to jump overboard? Swim your way to the ship?" Kane waived a hand at the water.

"Why did you chase me? Like an animal – like a madman!" The man asked, and at the word 'madman' he pressed his slight frame against the edge of the boat in anxiety. The small sinewy muscles in his thin arms were tensed like cords as his hands pushed against the edge of the wooden bench.

Kane gave him a wretched look.

"How long were you following us?"

The ragged man blinked, and did not answer. Kane sighed.

"How long were you following me?"

"Few days," the man said. He thought a moment and then nodded, as if in confirmation of this fact. "Saw you a couple times over the last few days."

"Then why didn't you say anything?" Kane asked. The man looked down for a moment to ponder the question and then back at Kane.

"Didn't know if you was one of us."

"Who else" – Kane wanted to shout but quelled his anger, and put his hand to his mouth – "Who else would I have been?"

"Don't know," the ragged man shrugged, "you could have been anyone in there," he said, pointing out over the water and to the jungle.

At this, however, Kane suddenly smiled. He looked towards where the man pointed, down into the dense greenery of the wild. The man was not wrong. In there he could have been anyone. Anyone he wanted. He could still hear some of the birds' songs and calls, though with each pull of the rowboat they grew softer. The leaves on the trees became indistinguishable and moment-by-moment the complexity of the jungle became simplified to groups of green, rock, beach and water.

Kane looked to the left of that shore with the four piles of bodies, to where he knew Bell lay buried. Then Kane shook his head at this thought. No, Bell was no more buried than those poor corpses on the shore were, and no more in the jungle than he himself was. No Bell was just gone – with him still, he knew, but gone nonetheless.

"Goodbye, old friend," Kane whispered.

Kane looked again upon the stretches of vast wilderness in either direction, growing larger and larger, unending. He thought of the many times he had left London, sailing down the Thames, leaving England behind him. What freedom he would feel, watching that river melt into the sea. Yet, leaving this coast, he felt that sense of freedom strip away with each pull of the oars.

The Marines rowed far enough out that Kane could see the mist drape the green hills that lay further inland. The tranquility of the jungle was ubiquitous, and reached across the water to Kane, permeating the unrest that he felt in his soul.

The allure and magnificence of this land would soon be gone, he knew. But it need not truly disappear. All he could do was appreciate it for these few moments longer, and keep that peace with him in the next land he ran aground.

As Kane leaned against the side of the rocking boat, watching that place he had called home these last weeks gradually shrink away from him, he smiled wistfully to himself. His future no longer lay here, he contemplated, but as the seeds of life find their way back to a cleared forest, or the birds may rebuild their once destroyed nest, so could he grow, rebuild, and live again.

Into the Jungle:
The Inspiration for *The Wreck*

In the spring of 2018, I had the good fortune to stay deep within a Costa Rican jungle for nearly a month. I was there to look after the pets of an off-grid vacation rental owner who had built tree house-style raised decks from the few trees that were cleared. There was no electricity, no internet, no walls. Only a mosquito net separated me from the natural world that was my surroundings.

To say I was profoundly shocked at the power and wonder that nature held would be an under-statement. It was a land almost completely untouched by humans, a world left to its own. It was there that I was able to experience the glory of the morning sun-rise, the estrangement of the nights, the hot humid days hiking down to the coast, and the swiftness and fury of the thunderstorms. Though, most of all, I was able to feel the otherworldly sensation of spending each day with nature, with only books and imagin-ation for entertainment. It was there that I felt, rather than understood, our connection with nature and its importance in our lives. It is a feeling I will never be able to shake.

I had begun writing the book there, in the jungle, with pen and paper. Later on, in the fall of 2018, I found myself in a different jungle. This time it was in Australia, backpacking and camping in its wild north where the story was ultimately finished. It was the culmination of all of these experiences, realizations, thoughts and adventures which I had hoped to express throughout *The Wreck*.